ONCE THE MULLAH

Once the Mullah

Persian folk tales

retold by
Alice Geer Kelsey
illustrated by
Kurt Werth

LONGMANS, GREEN AND CO.
New York • London • Toronto

LONGMANS, GREEN AND CO., INC.
55 FIFTH AVENUE, NEW YORK 3

LONGMANS, GREEN AND CO., LTD.
6 & 7 CLIFFORD STREET, LONDON W 1

LONGMANS, GREEN AND CO.
215 VICTORIA STREET, TORONTO 1

ONCE THE MULLAH

OCLC 1404952

COPYRIGHT · 1954
BY ALICE GEER KELSEY

PUBLISHED SIMULTANEOUSLY IN THE DOMINION OF CANADA BY
LONGMANS, GREEN AND CO., TORONTO

FIRST EDITION

LIBRARY OF CONGRESS CATALOG CARD NUMBER 54-8259

Printed in the United States of America

CONTENTS

FOREWORD

Have you read *Once the Hodja*? If you already know Nasr-ed-Din Hodja, I may not need to tell you what you will find in a book about a folk character named Mullah Nasr-ed-Din. (*Hodja* is the Turkish title for a Moslem priest who acts also as a teacher and a judge. *Mullah* is the Persian word for the same.) The people of Persia, a country that is called Iran in newspapers and geographies of today, love to laugh about their Mullah Nasr-ed-Din just as the people of Turkey love to laugh about their Nasr-ed-Din Hodja. Some of the stories told in the two countries are almost alike, with small differences that make them either Turkish or Persian. Other stories are special for one country or the other. There are hundreds of these folk tales.

In all these stories, Nasr-ed-Din—whether Hodja or Mullah—is a kindly old fellow with an impish sense of humor. He is quick to help anyone, though he is sometimes so awkward in his helping that he makes more trouble than he cures. He loves to play practical jokes, but his jokes never really hurt. He is always getting into tight

ix

places, but pulls through without losing his dignity. He makes mistake after mistake, but his village neighbors love and respect him just the same.

In Turkey it is said that Nasr-ed-Din Hodja lived at Ak Shehir at the time of Tamerlane the Great. In Iran I could learn no date nor home town for Mullah Nasr-ed-Din, perhaps because his stories may have been told first in Turkey. But it did seem important for Mullah Nasr-ed-Din to have a time and a place, so I chose a village near Isfahan in the sixteenth century. Isfahan then was the capital of Persia and the home of Shah Abbas the Great. If you visit Isfahan today you can see the beautiful mosques and palaces, the great square, and the wide streets built so long ago by Shah Abbas. The city still has its big covered bazaar. It still has its clever craftsmen famous for their work in silver, brass, copper, mosaics, and block printing.

Though the cities of modern Iran are changed in many ways from the Persian cities of the days of Mullah Nasr-ed-Din, village life is very much as described in these stories. There would be a few changes if we were writing about a village of Iran today. The men and boys would save their money (paper rials and paper tomans now) to buy bicycles. The rich Agha Abdul Karim would have an automobile, and the next-to-richest villagers would be thinking about owning one. The people would not depend for light on tallow candles or wicks in glasses of poppy-seed oil. They might have electric lights, and they surely would have kerosene lamps and perhaps gasoline lanterns. The big empty oil tins would be used for water jugs, flower pots, or patches on the front gate. The shops in the bazaar would have factory-made articles from away as well as the hand-made products of the community. The women would not be so careful about veiling their faces, but they would still find it convenient when leaving their homes to slip into an all-covering chuddar of factory-woven cloth, polka-dot design preferred. A village located on the main highway between cities would have buses passing through two or three times a day. There would often be a long-distance truck or a journeying car parked in front of the tea house.

But many things about village life are unchanged. The houses and garden walls are still made of the material nearest at hand, the local mud molded into bricks and dried in the sun. Trains of haughty camels still carry heavy loads, marching single file along the dusty roads. So do the patient little donkeys. Farmers still live in the village and go out by day to work their fields, vineyards, and orchards which belong to their landlord. Hens still wander about the village scavenging for food. Flocks of sheep and goats graze on the bristly growth of the untilled fields. Water for irrigating the fields and for village use flows through the ditches. The men and boys still gather on the slightest excuse while the women and girls hover in the background, always curious but never bold.

You may wonder how anyone collects folk stories in a foreign land. Fortunately many Persians speak English well, so we could use Nasr-ed-Din Hodja stories as bait for Mullah stories. A Hodja story would always remind someone of a Mullah story. Also there was a book of Mullah stories written in Persian, and boys who were learning English were glad to practise this language on us by putting these stories into English.

American boys and girls who live in Iran because of their fathers' work love to hear and tell Mullah stories. One eleven-year-old American boy tried to play a trick on me. When he found I was collecting Mullah stories for you, we swapped stories. I would tell him a Hodja story and he would top it with a Mullah story. When he ran out of real Mullah stories he tried telling "little moron" stories as though they happened to Mullah Nasr-ed-Din. But he could not fool me. The real Mullah has a wisdom all his own even when he is doing something that seems foolish. Anyone who knows Mullah Nasr-ed-Din would never confuse him with a moron.

I hope you will like Mullah Nasr-ed-Din. And I hope that these stories will remind you that people the world over like to laugh.

Alice Geer Kelsey

Tehran, Iran
August, 1953

ONCE THE MULLAH

DONKEY, MIND YOUR MOTHER!

HEE-HAW! Hee-haw!" sounded on every side of Mullah Nasr-ed-Din as he stood in the donkey bazaar of a long-ago Persian city. The donkey dealers crowded about him, each one trying to outshout the others. Every man had a different way of saying, "In all the world there is no better donkey than the one I am selling. And what a bargain!"

The Mullah stroked his gray beard and thought about the donkeys. His own small white donkey still served him well but she was growing old. A young donkey could do some of her work now and be ready to take her place when she grew too old to work.

The Mullah looked most important standing there, among the braying donkeys, in the white turban and long dark coat that marked him for priest, teacher, and judge of his village. The men in the donkey bazaar were eager to sell to him. Finally a white donkey pleased him. It had such a wise way of waggling its long velvety ears even though it was very young. Its bray told such a long, long story. It was pretty — white with a zigzag gray saddle mark on its back.

The Mullah bargained with the trader for a jolly half hour. All the good points of the donkey were made bigger and better as the dealer talked. All the bad points were made bigger and worse as the Mullah talked. Down a dinar at a time went the price the dealer demanded. Up a dinar at a time went the price the Mullah offered. At last the price met halfway. The seller, who was well pleased, beat his chest and vowed he had been robbed. The Mullah, who was delighted with his bargain, wrung his hands and groaned that *he* had been robbed. But both men were happy as the Mullah passed over the money and took the rope that was tied around the donkey's neck.

Throwing one leg over the back of his old donkey and slipping his arm through a loop of the new donkey's rope, the Mullah started off on the long ride to his own village. There was nothing new for him to see in the hot and treeless countryside — the same waving wheat fields, the same sheep and goats in their stubbly pasture, the same distant mountains with their traces of last winter's snow. The day was hot and growing hotter. The Mullah knew he could trust his faithful old donkey to jog home unguided toward her supper of straw. He tested the knots of the rope about the new donkey's neck. Then he did not even try to keep awake.

As he jounced along, fast asleep, he was joined by two rascals, an old man named Massoud and a boy named Suleiman. Both were strangers to the Mullah. They were riding their donkeys toward the city, looking for some mischief to do. They noticed how the Mullah's head bobbed in his sleep. They turned their donkeys' heads away from the city.

"That's a fine donkey the old mullah is leading," said Massoud in a loud whisper.

"It would bring a good price in the bazaar," young Suleiman whispered back.

"The mullah is dozing," said Massoud. "He would not notice if you and the young donkey changed places. You could slip your head through the rope and keep it taut. You could walk behind that old donkey, going clip-clip just like the young donkey. I could take the young donkey to the bazaar to sell."

"How about *you* and the donkey changing places," suggested the boy.

"Remember my lame foot!" Massoud was glad to think of such a good excuse. "An old man like me should not try to walk from here to the next village."

After a bit more of argument, Suleiman slipped the rope off the donkey's neck and tied it to a rope old Massoud carried. Then the boy stuck his own head through the rope held by the sleeping Mullah. Massoud rode his own donkey back to the bazaar leading Suleiman's gray donkey and the Mullah's young donkey with its zigzag gray saddle mark on its white coat. And Suleiman trudged along the road, the donkey's rope around his neck, breathing the chalky white dust stirred up by the small hoofs of the Mullah's old donkey.

Once in a while the Mullah's neck would stiffen as he wakened for a minute. He would feel the rope taut around his arm. He would hear steady footsteps behind him, clip-clip, clip-clip. All was well. Too sleepy to turn his head, the Mullah would doze off again.

It was when his old donkey stopped at his own street gate that Mullah Nasr-ed-Din woke up. Fatima lifted the latch in answer to his call. He rode inside with the proud air of a man who knows he has made a good bargain.

"See the fine donkey I bought in the bazaar in Isfahan," he called to his wife.

"What donkey?" She stared at Suleiman.

Seeing her surprise, the Mullah turned. For the first time he saw there was a boy where his new donkey had been. Suleiman was standing behind the old donkey, the rope still around his neck. He was wondering whether it would be a good idea to try to bray.

"Who are you?" shouted the Mullah. "And where is the fine young donkey I bought?"

"I am that donkey." Suleiman could think quickly when necessary and he had a story to tell. "I was a boy once before. I was changed into a donkey because I was always disobeying my mother. Belonging to such a good master as you, I was changed back to a boy again. Thank you, good Mullah, for doing this wonderful thing for me."

The Mullah stroked his beard. He did not know whether to be glad for the boy's good luck or sorry at the loss of the young donkey. "I paid many good dinars for you," he said at last, "but you are of no use to me. You may go free — on one condition."

"I will do anything for my freedom," promised Suleiman.

"You must promise to mind your mother. Go back to her as quickly as you can, and do whatever she tells you." The Mullah pointed his finger at Suleiman in his best teacher-judge manner. "Always obey your mother. Then you will keep out of trouble."

"I promise," vowed Suleiman solemnly. Then the Mullah slipped the rope from the boy's neck.

"Go," said the Mullah, "and may Allah bless you."

The next day Mullah Nasr-ed-Din had to go back to the bazaar to buy a new donkey to take the place of the one that had turned into a boy. Once again he stood in the donkey bazaar, stroking his gray beard and comparing donkeys. There were old donkeys and young donkeys, gray donkeys, black donkeys, white donkeys.

Suddenly the Mullah saw one that gave him quite

a start. It waggled its long velvety ears wisely in his direction. It brayed as though it had an especially long and interesting story to tell. And it was white with a zigzag gray saddle mark. It was the very donkey that he had bought yesterday. It was the donkey that had turned back into a boy. Now it was a donkey again.

In a whirl of flowing sleeves and streaming coat, the Mullah strode over to the donkey. He shook his finger at the little animal in his best teacher-judge manner.

"You bad boy!" he scolded. "You promised me that you would mind your mother! You disobeyed her again! Now see what has happened to you! You bad, bad boy!"

But the white donkey with the zigzag gray saddle mark only waggled its ears wisely and brayed.

MEAT OR CAT?

ONCE Mullah Nasr-ed-Din brought three kilos of meat to Fatima his wife. It was the best mutton to be found in the village bazaar. There was not a bit of waste on it — no bones, no chunks of fat — just good solid meat.

"I would like chulaw-kabab for dinner," he ordered. Then he started off on important business, as men so often do when there is extra work about the house.

Fatima went to work to make the chulaw-kabab. First she took the rice which had been soaking and put it in the big copper kettle to boil. Next she ground the meat till it was fine and soft as dough. She seasoned it with fresh herbs and garlic to just the tang her husband liked. Then she added flour and molded long narrow meat cakes ready to broil over her charcoal fire in the courtyard.

When it was nearly time for the hungry Mullah to come home, sniffing for chulaw-kabab, she strung the meat cakes on the sharp kabob iron and turned them round and round over the charcoal fire. How good it smelled, that best of mutton seasoned to the taste of the Mullah! Its fragrance wafted over the mud walls to the neighbors. East to Ina, sitting at her loom to knot her red and blue rug. West to Turan, putting her loaves of dark bread into her outdoor oven heated by burning twigs. South to Setare, sitting in her garden hoping for a cool breeze. The sizzling kabob told each of these women, alone behind her own mud walls, that other women were behind other mud walls. To each woman came the urge to talk and to listen. Each one pulled close her long homespun chuddar that covered her from head to toe, and slipped quietly through her own street gate. At almost the same moment the three women knocked on Fatima's door. Gladly she opened to them and joined in the chatter as they sat cross-legged about the charcoal fire drinking glasses of sweet hot tea.

They were still laughing and gossiping together when the kabob was cooked tender and the rice puffed its fullest. Fatima was a good hostess. She knew that second glasses of tea would be slim hospitality when the air was full of the good smell of chulaw-kabab.

"They will not eat much," she convinced herself as she bustled into the house for a platter. "There will be plenty left for the Mullah's dinner."

Fatima laid the broiled meat on the platter. She covered it with fluffy rice and poured melted butter over it all. She was rightly proud of her cooking. The four women sat on the ground around the steaming platter. They dipped daintily with their fingers and started eating.

Fatima was right that they would not eat much —

rice. They helped themselves generously to the well-seasoned meat cakes.

"What a good cook you are!" said Ina between bites.

"You must let me watch you make chulaw-kabab some day." Turan reached for more. "Mine is never as good as this."

"I thought I could cook rice, but yours is drier than mine." But it was more meat than rice that Setare took as she scooped again from the platter.

Fatima beamed at their praise. She urged them to take more. Being a gracious hostess seemed more important right then than being a good wife. Soon the last shred of meat was gone. Ina remembered the rug on her loom waiting in her own house. Turan remembered the bread baking in her outdoor oven. Setare remembered that it was time to water her flower garden. With polite invitations to visit them soon, the three neighbors pulled their chuddars modestly over their faces and went back behind their own mud walls.

There was just time for Fatima to arrange the remnants of rice on a smaller platter before she heard the clip-clip of the Mullah's trotting donkey. She lifted the latch of the street gate to let her husband ride into the courtyard.

"Mmmmmmm," he sniffed as he gave his donkey some straw to munch. "That chulaw-kabab smells good! What a cook you are, my jewel among wives!"

He joined Fatima sitting cross-legged on one of her hand-knotted Persian rugs. There was at each place a blue bowl of fresh mast, a large chunk of bread, and a cucumber cool from the well. And between them there was a platter heaped with rice that was yellow with melted butter and powdered saffron. The Mullah could see no meat, but he was sure it was hidden under the fluffy rice. Couldn't he smell it spicing the air?

When he dipped his hand into the heap of rice, he expected to find plenty of meat cakes. Nothing but rice! He dove in with both hands. Still nothing but rice! The best of husbands, when hungry, can endure only so much.

"What does this mean?" he shouted at Fatima. "I gave you three kilos of meat to make chulaw-kabab. The house and yard smell of broiled mutton, but you feed me only rice. *Where is the meat?*"

Fatima trembled. She did not dare tell about Ina, Turan, and Setare. The Mullah was in such a rage that he might dash over to their houses and start fights with their husbands. Fatima remembered the words in the Koran about telling a lie to prevent trouble between friends. She could never learn that every lie she told just led her deeper into trouble. She glanced wildly about the room trying to think what story she could tell her husband.

She saw her yellow cat dozing on the sunny door-step. If the cat had been somewhere else at that minute, the Mullah's wife might have told the truth. But the cat made her think of such a good story to tell.

"The cat!" She pointed at it, twitching its tail as it dreamed of mice. "The cat grabbed the meat and ate every bit of it while I was going to the well for the cucumbers. It was licking the meat juice from its whiskers when I came back."

The Mullah looked from cat to wife — from wife to cat — from cat to wife again. The dozing cat seemed her usual long and scrawny self. His red-faced wife looked as though she would be glad of an earthquake, robbers, fire — anything to turn the Mullah's eyes from her.

He walked slowly to the corner where he kept the scales that he used to weigh mulberries or pomegranates from his saddlebags in the bazaar. Carefully he laid three of the kilo weights on one tray of the scales. Solemnly he laid the sleepy yellow cat on the balancing tray. It was so dozy that it curled in the new position with only a small twitch of ears and whiskers. The Mullah lifted the scales in air. He held them steadily while they wavered and swayed. They came to a stop at an even balance between the three kilo weights and the cat.

"The meat weighed just three kilos." The Mullah's voice was so stern that Fatima decided never to speak anything but the truth again. "Now the cat weighs three kilos."

"Just three kilos," echoed the red-faced Fatima.

"If I am weighing the cat, where is the meat?" asked the Mullah. "And if I am weighing the meat, where is the cat?"

And poor Fatima did not even try to answer that question.

POMEGRANATES FOR SALE

MULLAH NASR-ED-DIN was proud of the bushy pomegranate tree that grew within the mud walls that surrounded his house and garden. He loved to watch the red blossoms growing among the glossy green leaves. He loved to see the round green balls swell as their tufts of blossoms shrivelled. He watered them every day from the garden pool that was kept filled from the ditch beside the village street.

Pomegranate harvest was a proud time for the Mullah. He was sure that his pomegranates were as fine as the famous ones grown near Qum. He picked each of the shining red balls separately, never shaking them into a blanket as some of his careless neighbors did. He stored what could be eaten at home. Then he loaded the rest into the saddle baskets balanced one on either side of his little white donkey. Then Mullah and donkey plodded along the dusty road to the nearby city of Isfahan.

"Ai anar," he shouted the name of his fruit as he walked through the streets of Isfahan. He did not call his wares often till he reached the center of the city. It would be too bad to sell all the pomegranates before he had the fun of mingling with other merchants in the great square with its pool and its polo field. The Mullah liked being a merchant for a day. He could forget his mosque, his wriggling schoolboys, and his neighbors with arguments for him to settle.

"Ai anar," he called as he guided his donkey. Only three marketing housewives had peered from behind their chuddars to bargain for pomegranates before he reached the center of town. His saddle baskets were still heaped with the red fruit when he took up his stand near the entrance of the great covered bazaar with its network of shop-lined alleys. From where he stood, he could look across the great square at Ali Kapou, the Shah's palace. Behind it were the royal gardens and the other royal buildings. Perhaps the Shah himself might be sitting on his high veranda with its many pillars decorated with mirrors and inlaid work.

Thinking of the Shah, the Mullah put more vim into his voice as he called his pomegranates for sale.

"Ai anar! Ai anar! Ripe, sweet, red, and juicy! Ai anar! Ai anar!" The Mullah loved the sound of his voice. He knew it was as rich and clear as it was when it rang out from the minaret of his own village mosque.

"Ai anar! Ai anar!" called the Mullah.

Suddenly he had a rude interruption.

"Hee-haw! Hee-haw!" brayed his donkey in a voice even more loud and clear than her master's. The Mullah glared at the interfering donkey, but said nothing. He waited till the donkey's bray faded on the air.

"Ai anar! Ai anar!" called the Mullah again. He winced to see his donkey bracing her small feet and curling back her long lips.

"Hee-haw! Hee-haw!" The donkey's bray rose and fell, wave upon wave, while the Mullah's face turned redder than his own pomegranates. There was silence again.

"Ai anar! Ai anar!" The Mullah's voice cracked.

"Hee-haw! Hee-haw!" brayed the donkey. "Hee-haw! Hee-haw!" again and again.

Snickering children crowded around them. The chuddars of veiled women shook as though their wearers, deep under the folds of cloth, were laughing with the children. A donkey on the other side of the great square gave an answering bray. Men, forgetting they had business in the covered bazaar, stopped to look, to listen, and to jest.

"Ai anar! Ai anar!" called the Mullah in a voice that was growing faint. He cast a nervous eye toward Ali Kapou, hoping that the Shah was not sitting on his high veranda between the tall columns.

"Hee-haw! Hee-haw!" This last bray was just one more than the Mullah could endure. Red-faced with

shame and anger, he grabbed the donkey's long nose, even while her lips were opening to bray again. The Mullah pulled it around so he could glare straight into the little animal's eye.

"Tell me, miserable and impudent donkey," he shouted, "are *you* selling these pomegranates, or am *I*?"

Then the crowd, laughing, bought pomegranates as fast as the Mullah could weigh them and put the clinking dinars in his money bag.

THE MULLAH'S OVEN

MULLAH NASR-ED-DIN tried to give his wife what she wanted, even if pleasing her meant work for him.

"I am tired of going to the village oven to bake my bread," complained Fatima. "Some of my friends have ovens in their own yards. Setare's husband built her a fine one of clay. Turan has an oven. So does Ina."

"I will build an oven for you," promised the Mullah. Let it not be said that other husbands did more for their wives than he did for Fatima.

He worked for days, during the cooler hours, making clay bricks. He molded them and set them on edge in the sun to bake. He worked all one day, except for naptime under the mulberry tree, putting the bricks together in a smooth round-topped oven. He made it with a deep hole which Fatima could fill with burning twigs before she put in her loaves and closed the door to bake them. The oven was almost finished by evening, and a very fine one it was.

The Mullah was admiring it when neighbor Mehmet Ali the coppersmith strolled through the gate to have an evening chat. The visitor stared at the oven, first from one side and then from the other. He scowled and shook his head. "Puh, puh, puh!" he murmured.

"What is the matter with my oven?" asked the Mullah.

"It faces *east*," sighed Mehmet Ali.

"And why should it not face east?" asked the Mullah.

Mehmet Ali's voice was full of gloom as he answered, "Have you never noticed which way the wind usually blows? With your oven facing east, the wind will put out your fire before you can start it!"

Next morning the Mullah tore the oven to pieces and built it over again, facing west. He worked hard all day, except of course for the hot hours of early afternoon when he stretched on the ground for a nap. By evening the oven was finished again. Mullah Nasr-ed-Din was standing back the better to admire it when he heard a tap at the street gate.

In came neighbor Daoud the farmer. "So you've

been building an oven," he said, examining it.

"And a very fine oven it is." The Mullah beamed, turning to his friend for the praise he knew the oven deserved.

Daoud squinted at the oven, first with one eye and then with the other. He frowned. He tapped his foot in displeasure. He murmured under his breath, "Puh, puh, puh!"

"What is the matter with my oven?" The Mullah's voice was small and worried.

"It faces *west*," sighed Daoud.

"Why should it not face west?" asked the Mullah.

"Surely you have noticed which way the wind usually blows!" Daoud's voice was full of pain that the Mullah could be so careless. "There will never be enough draft to start a fire in an oven that faces west. Puh, puh, puh!"

Next morning the Mullah tore his beautiful oven down again. This time he rebuilt it on an old cart with two wooden wheels. He worked hard all day, even making his nap shorter than usual. By evening the oven was so nearly finished that he took time to stop and admire it.

Just then Mehmet Ali and Daoud together strolled through Mullah Nasr-ed-Din's gate for a chat with him, and perhaps for another look at what he was building. Together they stared at the new oven built on its cart. They walked round it and round it. They touched the wheels to be sure they could believe what their eyes told them.

Mehmet Ali asked, "Why, oh why . . . ?"

And Daoud finished his question, "Why did you build your oven on top of a cart?"

The Mullah smiled contentedly as he answered, "I built it on a cart with wooden wheels so that I can turn it in any direction — north, south, east, or west — whichever way my neighbors want it to face."

UP AND DOWN THE MINARET

MULLAH NASR-ED-DIN gazed up at the hot sun. It was almost directly overhead. Only a few minutes were left before he had to be at the top of the tall minaret. Soon his voice must ring out over all the city in the midday call to prayer. He clucked to his small white donkey who promptly changed from a slow walk to a slow jog.

The Mullah was proud that he had been chosen to give the call from the tall minaret of great Mosque Jameh when the regular muezzin of that mosque was sick. The Mullah was used to giving the call to prayer from the low minaret of the tiny mosque of his own small village at the edge of Persia's capital city of Isfahan. Then he was heard by only a hundred families, all old friends. It did not matter if his voice did crack a bit on the high notes. Perhaps his call from the minaret of Mosque Jameh would be so full and clear that the Shah would invite him to chant the call from the minaret of the royal mosque with its vaulted tiled dome of lapis lazuli, turquoise, and gold.

Mullah Nasr-ed-Din had made special preparations for this great day. His gray beard was washed and combed. The white turban wound around his bald head was as clean as Fatima could pound it with a flat stick in the ditch that brought water to his village. His long undercoat had been washed and his sleeveless overcoat of dark wool had only the dust that had collected as he rode from home.

The sun had not quite touched the top of the sky when he slid off his donkey by the great mosque with its brick-vaulted dome between tall minarets. Wiping the sweat from his face with the long sleeve of his undercoat, the Mullah walked jauntily through the door into the nearest minaret. A bit of the jauntiness left him as he looked up the spiral staircase twisting up, up, up. At first, coming in from the brightness of midday, he could see only dimly. But as his eyes grew used to the half darkness, it seemed that the stairs wound upward forever. If he were going to be mullah of this mosque, he would surely train his donkey to carry him up those endless stairs!

He wished he could sit down for a good rest before

starting up those hundreds of steps, but he remembered how high the sun was. The midday call to prayer must ring out. So, lifting his long-skirted coat, he started the weary upward twist. Step — step — step. Puff — puff — puff. Would he never reach the top? He felt almost homesick for the low minaret of his village with its spiral staircase that he could climb in two good breaths. On he went. Step — step — step. Puff — puff — puff.

At last he came out into the sunshine of the balcony just under the sharp tip of the minaret. As he leaned on the railing to get back his breath before chanting the call to prayer, he looked down to see the dizzy height he had climbed.

And there, far below him on the ground, stood a raggedly dressed man who was gesturing wildly at him.

"Come down here! In the name of Allah, come down," called the shabby man. "I have something important to tell you!"

"I am listening," the Mullah yelled back. "Shout it up to me!"

"Impossible," was the answer. "I must speak to you here, where we can talk eye to eye."

"First I will chant the call to prayer," yelled Mullah

Nasr-ed-Din. "Then I can come down to talk with you."

"That will never do," the man shouted. "What I have to say cannot wait. Come down here now, I beg of you."

"I must give the call to prayer first." Mullah Nasr-ed-Din cupped his mouth with his hand, leaned forward, and took a long breath — ready for the midday call to prayer. But as he leaned forward, he could see nothing but the ragged man below, motioning and shouting as though every life in Isfahan depended on what he must whisper privately in the ear of Mullah Nasr-ed-Din.

The Mullah looked again at the sun. Allah would not care, perhaps, if prayers rose to him a few minutes late today. The man's message might really be important. It might be from the Shah himself. The ragged man did not look like the bearer of important messages, but one never could be sure.

With a shiver and a sigh the Mullah looked at the spiral staircase winding down, down, down into the darkness. At least he could hurry on the downward trip without losing his breath. Round and round he ran, holding his long-skirted garments high to keep from catching as he whirled around the curves. He felt light-headed. There was a flutter in his stomach that seemed like a giggle coming.

At last he stepped out into the sunlight and leaned against the minaret till the city stopped whirling about him. When the trees and the buildings stood solidly on their own roots and foundations, he found himself looking into the open hand of the man who had called him down from the minaret.

"I am hungry," whined the man in the voice of

one who makes his living by begging. "My wife is sick. My seven children are hungry. Allah will reward you richly for anything you give me."

Mullah Nasr-ed-Din stared at the beggar. Had he hurried down that long curling staircase to listen to a beggar's whine? He could hear that any day at any street corner. For a minute the Mullah was too shocked to speak, too shocked to think. Then he had an idea.

He leaned closer to the beggar to say in his most impressive voice, "Climb to the top of the minaret with me."

"Oh, no," said the beggar. "You can give me the money right here."

"Impossible," said the Mullah. He made his voice lower than before to repeat, "Come up to the top of the minaret with me."

The beggar dropped his outstretched hand, the better to wonder what to do. He was being asked to use some effort to get money. He wanted it to fall into his hand without any work on his part. It was a long climb up the minaret, but it might be worth while. There was no knowing what treasure the Mullah might have up there. The Mullah's pleased smile must mean good news.

Mullah Nasr-ed-Din said, "Follow me," and started up the long spiral staircase. This time he could do it with only a little huffing and puffing. His climb up and down had limbered him. And perhaps this trip was easier because he was chuckling over the surprise he would give the beggar when they reached the balcony of the minaret. At last the two men were out in the sunshine. The Mullah stood straight while the beggar leaned against the railing, puffing for breath.

"Now what was it you were asking me?" The Mullah used a soft, kind voice.

Out went the beggar's hand. "Allah bless you, good Mullah, for taking pity on a hungry man. My sick wife will pray for you. My seven hungry children will ask Allah to bless you. You see my empty hand before you. Fill it, good Mullah, fill it!"

"You have climbed the minaret to get my answer." Mullah Nasr-ed-Din stroked his gray beard. The man wriggled the fingers of his begging hand hopefully. His whining beggar's tale went on and on.

"I wait your answer, good Mullah," whined the beggar. His open hand fairly trembled in eagerness.

Then the Mullah stood his tallest to shout, "My answer is No!"

As the beggar slunk down the staircase, Mullah Nasr-ed-Din leaned on the railing. He cupped his mouth with his hand and chanted the call to prayer. He chanted with the loud, clear voice of a man who is sure of himself. Hadn't he taught a good lesson to the beggar whose feet he could hear dragging scuff-scuff-scuff down the long staircase?

TREASURE IN THE BASKET

MULLAH NASR-ED-DIN heard dragging footsteps outside the mud walls that surrounded his
house and garden. It was Thursday, the day when the
Mullah stayed in his house of mud bricks or in his
garden full of the flowers he loved to weed and
water. The gate that opened through his walls into
the village street would be unlocked all that day.
His neighbors knew that they could walk through
that gate at any time on Thursdays to talk with him.
On Fridays he would be at the mosque. On other
days he might be teaching wriggling boys to read
the Holy Koran, or he might be riding off on donkeyback for business of his own. But on Thursdays he
belonged to his village neighbors.

The dragging footsteps stopped by the Mullah's
gate. There was a hesitating knock.

"Come in!" welcomed Mullah Nasr-ed-Din. The
gate opened and a gloomy-faced man stepped slowly

inside. "Salam, Abdul Ali," the Mullah greeted him.

"Salam," answered Abdul Ali's tired voice. Then he asked polite questions about the Mullah's health. The Mullah guessed he had come for more than that.

"How can I serve you, Abdul Ali?" The Mullah stroked his gray beard thoughtfully, wondering what bad luck had overtaken the man this time.

"I am in great trouble, Mullah Nasr-ed-Din!" Abdul Ali beat his breast with both hands to show how he was suffering. "Just when my figs were ripe, a heavy wind knocked them from the tree. They are too bruised to load in my donkey's saddlebags to carry to market. I was depending on those figs for money to buy flour and rice and olive oil. Now my poor family will be hungry till grape harvest."

The Mullah looked at him keenly. Was he telling the truth? Well, hungry children were hungry children.

"See that basket on the high shelf in the corner." The Mullah pointed. "There is money in that basket for just such times as this. Take what you need."

"I will take only as much as I need," said Abdul Ali as he emptied every coin from the basket into his money bag. "I'll return every dinar, with interest, as soon as I harvest my grapes and sell them."

"Good!" The Mullah walked with him to the street gate. "That basket is for people who need it. It does not fill itself. When you put the money back, there will be something for the next person who needs it."

"Depend on me!" promised Abdul Ali, though his mind was more on spending the money in his bag than on returning it for someone else to use. "I will be back with this amount, and more, on the very day that I sell my grapes."

"May Allah bless you!" said the Mullah as he watched him pass through the gate and turn toward the bazaar to buy flour and rice and olive oil.

But the grape season passed and Abdul Ali did not return. Another grape season passed, and another, and another. Still Abdul Ali had not put a single dinar back in the basket he had emptied.

It was on a Thursday, four years later, that the Mullah heard the same dragging footsteps outside his unlocked gate. He heard the same hesitating knock. In answer to the Mullah's hearty "Come in" the gate opened. In walked Abdul Ali.

The Mullah started to thank him for coming to return the money. Then, because he was very wise, the Mullah waited to let his guest speak first.

The two men talked about each other's health, about the crops, about the Shah's latest decree. At first Abdul Ali seemed nervous. He acted as though he feared the Mullah might mention something unpleasant — returning borrowed money, for instance. As they talked, with no sign from the Mullah that he remembered what had happened four years ago, Abdul Ali relaxed. He could laugh in a melancholy sort of way at the Mullah's jokes. Fatima brought them glasses of hot tea which they sipped through lumps of sugar held between their teeth. Abdul Ali was sure now that his host had forgotten about the borrowed money. So, when the Mullah asked, "Is there anything I can do for you?" the guest dared ask for money again.

"I am in great trouble," sighed Abdul Ali. "No man works harder than I. But fate is against me. My milch goat died. We have no milk for soup, and no mast to eat with our bread. I must have money to buy a new goat."

"See that basket on the high shelf in the corner? That is where I keep money to help people who are in trouble." The Mullah did not need to point at the basket this time. Abdul Ali was taking it off the shelf before the Mullah had finished speaking. He looked in the basket. He ran his hand around inside it. He felt of the spot on the shelf where the basket had stood.

"There is no money here!" Abdul Ali looked accusingly at the Mullah.

"Are you sure?" The Mullah scuffed across the room to look in the basket too. Together the two men shook the basket, searched on the floor, stood on tiptoe to look on the shelf.

"Puh, puh, puh!" was the Mullah's way of showing how disappointed and displeased he was. Then he added, slowly so that Abdul Ali could not possibly miss a word, "Of course, if you had put back the money that you took from the basket, there would be something for you now."

In less than a minute Abdul Ali was going out the street gate, but he could not go fast enough to escape the Mullah's warning, "Life is like that basket. A man cannot always be taking and never giving. Neither lives nor baskets fill themselves with treasure."

THE HEAD OF THE FAMILY

ONCE Mullah Nasr-ed-Din was dinner guest in the home of Agha Abdul Karim, the chief rug merchant in the village near the edge of Isfahan. If the fine house and large garden had failed to tell the Mullah that there was good money in buying and selling the carpets knotted by the clever fingers of the women and children, his host would have made it plain. From the minute a servant ushered the Mullah into the room where Agha Abdul Karim sat cross-legged on a silky Persian carpet, the merchant talked about his own success. He seemed to forget the honor due the Mullah's priestly robe and turban. He forgot that his guest was a person of importance also.

When Agha Abdul Karim tired of proving that he was the head of the rug business for the entire Isfahan area, he began bragging about his family. Obviously he was head of his household also. "I told my wife . . ." "I gave my sons permission . . ." "I plan for my daughters . . ." On and on and on.

The merchant was proud of his family too. When his wife would flit quietly across a corner of the room, he would say, "My Jamileh! How we all depend on her! I am of course the head of this family, but it is Jamileh who holds us together."

When his daughters would slip silently through the room, peering from under their veils at the Mullah, their father would look lovingly after them and sigh, "My Akhtar and my Nadereh! They are the hands of their mother. Never did two girls stand by a mother more ready to help. They are jewels among daughters."

And when his two sturdy sons romped into sight, the merchant would pat them proudly on the shoulders and say, "My Jamshid and my Rustam! They are growing up to be the props of my old age. Already our whole family rests on them for support." And the Mullah, who was very wise, did not tell his host what mischievous and wriggling props Jamshid and Rustam were when they sat in his schoolroom studying the Holy Koran.

Mullah Nasr-ed-Din was willing to hear about Agha Abdul Karim's success part of the time, but not all the time. He thought the rug merchant might stop talking once in a while and let him take a turn. He had plenty of his own bragging he would like to do. Whenever Agha Abdul Karim stopped for breath, Mullah Nasr-ed-Din opened his mouth to take over. But the host needed such short breathers that the Mullah could never get a tongue-hold on conversation.

By the time Jamileh and her two jewels among daughters were fluttering about the servants who were bringing in dinner, the Mullah was utterly miserable. To have so much to say but no chance to say it! To have to listen to story after story about Agha Abdul Karim's work and family when he had so much to say about his own! Could there be a more torturing way to spend an evening?

The servants set the huge copper tray between the two men on the carpet of brightest Isfahan red. They brought in seven bowls of soup made of mast and cucumbers.

"I am not like the heads of most households," explained Agha Abdul Karim. "My wife and daughters eat with me. Because you are only a mullah, they can come to the table as usual tonight. I will even let them lift their veils to eat."

After the first course of soup, there was a second

course of broiled eggplant. Then the servants brought
in a big platter of rice pilau and a small platter holding one chicken roasted and served complete from
beak to claws.

"Our honored guest will carve and divide the
chicken," announced Agha Abdul Karim. The
Mullah could see he was pleased with himself. Now
the rug merchant need not politely take a poor piece
of chicken for himself.

The Mullah picked up the carving knife. He
counted the six people and remembered that he made
seven. He knew how to divide a small chicken between himself and Fatima ever so neatly, with some
left over for tomorrow's soup. But to divide a chicken
into seven pieces of proper size was a real problem
for the Mullah who knew more about the Koran than
he knew about arithmetic.

The hungry Mullah waved his knife uncertainly
over the chicken. The voice of Agha Abdul Karim
ran on. "Of course usually I carve the chicken my-
self, as head of the family."

"As head of the family . . ." repeated the Mullah.
Suddenly he knew how he would carve and serve the
chicken. "As head of the family, you deserve a suit-
able part of the meat."

The host smiled contentedly as he fixed his eye on a plump side of breast meat — surely the proper piece for him.

"As head of the family," repeated the Mullah with his most innocent smile, "you deserve the head of the chicken." With a quick slash he cut off the fowl's gaunt head. The beak clicked dully as it fell on the plate of the amazed Agha Abdul Karim.

"Your wife, as you have said so many times, holds your whole family together. What could be better

meat for her than the neck of the chicken that holds head to body." Sure of himself now, the Mullah flicked his knife to cut off the neck and toss it on Jamileh's plate. The poor woman was all too used to eating chicken necks, but she had hoped for a bit of white meat when the good Mullah carved.

"Now for your two lovely daughters who are the hands for their mother." The Mullah slashed at the first wing. "The wings of a chicken are its hands. One for you, Nadereh! And a nice crisp one for you, Akhtar!" The girls looked hungrily at the meaty body of the chicken and then at the bony wings the Mullah had plopped on their plates. Nadereh, who had the happy gift of seeing the funny side of life, glanced quickly at her father's red face. Then she smiled demurely into her veil.

"Now for the two props of the family, the supports on which the home rests." The Mullah sliced off the two legs of the chicken. "One for you, Jamshid! The other for you, Rustam!"

For once Agha Abdul Karim was speechless. His family, used to letting him do the talking, merely sat and gazed from platter to plates. It was still the Mullah's chance to talk.

"Nothing left but the body," sighed the Mullah

as he piled the rest of the chicken on his own plate.
"All the important parts are gone, all the parts that
have a special meaning. But I am only a mullah.
What is left will be good enough for me."

Then for a change nobody talked. Mullah Nasr-
ed-Din was too busy comparing one delicious morsel
of chicken with another, smothering great mouth-
fuls in the well-cooked pilau. Jamileh and her four
children avoided the eyes of the head of the family.
And Agha Abdul Karim had nothing to say — ab-
solutely nothing.

THE QUILT

IT WAS a hot night, much too hot to sleep in the house with its small high windows. Mullah Nasr-ed-Din and his good wife had carried their mattress onto the roof where they could catch any breezes that might blow their way. They had brought with them one of the patchwork quilts that Fatima had made with her own careful stitches. They might need to pull it over themselves in the cool of the morning, just before the sun pinkened the sky behind the mountains. The stars were golden bright in the moonless sky, seeming very close to the people who lay on mattresses looking upward.

Fatima and the Mullah had been asleep a short time when they were wakened by loud noises in the street below them. Mingled with the angry voices of quarreling men, they could hear the thud of heavy sticks. There was the creak and bang of opening gates as many neighbors peeked out to see what was happening. There was the padding of hurrying feet as men ran out to join the fight on whichever side struck their fancy.

"If I were a man," chided Fatima, "I would be out there in the street finding out what all the fuss is about. I would not be lying in bed on my own safe rooftop."

The Mullah's sense of curiosity was second only to Fatima's. He needed no more urging. Whatever was going on, he wanted to be in the midst of it, helping and advising. No doubt the wisdom of the village judge was needed out there.

He was in too great a hurry to go into the house for his coat and turban. He threw the patchwork quilt over his shoulders and wriggled his feet into his slippers with their turned-up toes and their turned-down heels. Then he scurried down the narrow stairs that led from roof to ground. His gate creaked as he ran into the street, his quilt fluttering and flapping behind him.

"What's going on?" he shouted. He ran toward the tangle of quarreling men, raising his voice louder and louder. "Stop fighting! Go back to your homes! Stop fighting this minute, I say!"

But the fighting men were in no mood to be told

what to do. Their fight had gone too far. Even a
mullah in robe and turban could not have stopped
their punching and shouting. What chance had a
bald mullah wrapped in a patchwork quilt?

"Go back home yourself!" shouted one of the
men as the crowd turned on the Mullah. They tapped
his bald head with their sticks. They threw small
stones at him. They grabbed his quilt and pulled.
Some tugged in one direction and some pulled in
another. It was a strong quilt made of homespun
cotton pieces and sewed with Fatima's best stitches,
but it was not strong enough for such a struggle.
There was the dull sound of ripping in the darkness
as piece after piece tore off in the hands of one man
after another. When the Mullah finally squirmed
away, there was only enough quilt left to make a
ragged collar round his neck. He limped away without waiting to give any more advice.

Candle in hand, Fatima met her hero at the gate.
She was sorry for her battered husband, but her curiosity was stronger than her pity.

"What was the fighting about?" she asked.

"Oh, not much of anything." The Mullah rubbed
his bruised head and pushed past her inside the gate.
"The men were only quarreling over my quilt!"

THE SADDLE

ONCE Mullah Nasr-ed-Din went a journey on donkeyback. He jogged along between fields barren except for the coarse camel thorn. He met a train of slow-stepping camels, a shepherd driving his black goats in search of pasture, a traveling merchant carrying his wares in saddlebags at his donkey's sides, a rich man's wife riding in a horse-drawn carriage with curtains shielding her from the world, and two of the Shah's soldiers riding white horses. But most of the time the road stretched dusty-white and empty ahead of him. Most of the time there was no motion other than the flight of a vulture, the swift bounding of a gazelle, or the twisting of dust-whirls here and there in the wilderness. The Mullah watched the sun climb high till it was directly overhead.

"Time for midday prayer," the Mullah reminded himself. "Where can I find water to wash before prayer?" He rode on hoping for some water that would not turn out to be only a mirage when he reached it. At last he found a brown stream running slowly in a deep irrigation ditch a short distance from the road.

The Mullah took off his coat and threw it over the donkey's back. The flowing sleeves and long skirt of his priestly coat would be in his way when he stooped to wash in the irrigation ditch. The donkey drooped her head and fell asleep. The Mullah slid down the clay bank toward the water.

He was so busy with his washing that he did not notice the clip-clip of another donkey's feet passing

on the dusty road. First the Mullah washed his hands three times. Then he washed his face three times. Above the splashing of the water he did not hear that the second donkey hesitated beside his own. He never suspected that its rider reached out and grabbed the coat the Mullah had dropped on his donkey's back for safe-keeping. Three times the Mullah washed his arms, never hearing the faster trot as the thief urged his donkey into a run. The water was so cool that he splashed noisily and hummed a loud tune to himself as he washed. He took off his white turban and washed the place where his hair used to be, never hearing the hoof beats of the strange donkey fade into nothingness in the distance.

The Mullah took his prayer stone from his pocket and laid it in front of him, toward Mecca. He bowed to the waist while he recited prayers from the Koran. Then he kneeled and touched his forehead to the sacred stone as he recited more prayers. The Mullah's prayers took longer than those of some men because he knew all of the Koran and loved every singing word of it. Unlike his neighbors, he knew the meaning of the Arabic words, at least some of them. He had studied well in the school for mullahs at the blue-domed mosque on the Street of the Four Gardens in Isfahan. On and on went his prayers. He could chant as well by the roadside as in the village mosque. Allah, the Creator of all things made the wilderness also. Allah could hear the Mullah's voice wherever it rose.

"Now if you ask them, Who created the heavens and earth?
certainly they will say, Created were they by the Mighty, the All-Knowing.
He fashioned for you the earth as a cradle,
* and fashioned for you therein roads;*
*   perchance you will go the right way."*

At last his prayers were over. At peace with the world, he clambered from the ditch back up to the road and his patient little donkey. Then came a shock. The quiet mystic mood of his prayers vanished. His coat was gone!

The Mullah looked up the road. He looked down the road. He looked out over the flat wilderness that rolled brown to the foot of the mountains that rimmed the plain. Not a living creature was in sight except a brown lizard hunting for insects and the Mullah's own donkey having its midday nap. The coat could not have been wafted up into the skies.

Someone must have taken it. The Mullah stared at his donkey, looking so innocent with her sleeping head almost dragging in the dust. There was no one else.

The Mullah grabbed the donkey by the bridle. "Give me back my coat, you thieving beast," he shouted.

The donkey shook herself awake. She pulled back her long upper lip and brayed a sleepy "Hee-haw" which sounded like a yawn.

"Yes, pretend you were asleep. Make believe you know nothing about my coat," stormed the Mullah. "I trusted you to take care of it. Where have you hidden it?"

The donkey's silence enraged the Mullah even more than her braying. She turned her long velvety ears toward him as though asking what all the shouting was about. The more surprised and innocent she acted, the angrier grew the Mullah. He stamped back and forth, shouting at the donkey till at last he thought of a way to get even with her.

He untied the donkey's saddle and clapped it on his own back. Awkwardly he fastened it across his chest and tied it under his chin. It flopped uncomfortably on his back, but the Mullah felt better. He was giving his donkey the punishment she deserved.

"See, you thieving donkey!" scolded the Mullah. "You took my coat. Now I have taken your saddle."

The donkey twitched her white hide at the freedom from the heavy, hot saddle. But she answered never a single "Hee-haw!"

"Don't ask to have your saddle back again," scolded the Mullah. "You won't have it till you give me my own coat. And don't complain to me. You have taken my coat and I have taken your saddle to wear in its place. That is only fair. Now start for home."

The donkey brayed cheerfully and pranced off, as cool and free as she would be if she were grazing with the village herds. Behind the donkey stumbled Mullah Nasr-ed-Din wearing the heavy saddle in place of the stolen coat. As he plodded along, stooping under his load, he kept mumbling in a voice that grew smaller and fainter, "I'll wear this saddle till you give me back my coat, you thief of a donkey."

A DINAR FOR A DONKEY

ONE day Mullah Nasr-ed-Din went to the little mud-brick stable built against the corner of his walled garden. He planned to saddle his small donkey and jog to the other end of the village to visit one of his friends. To his horror the stable was empty.

Hunting for the donkey the Mullah dashed round and round within his own walls so furiously that he lost one of his floppy shoes, caught his white turban on a low branch, and tore the loose sleeve of his long coat on the prickles of a berry bush. Then he noticed that the street gate was swinging, unlatched.

"Where is my donkey?" he shouted as he ran out his street gate. Passers-by joined in the search. Everyone knew that Mullah Nasr-ed-Din without his small white donkey would be lost indeed. They ran through the streets. They ran up and down the narrow alleys. They knocked on doors and asked if anyone had seen the Mullah's donkey. They ran to the edge of the village walls and studied all the roads leading to the outside world. Everyone wanted to help.

The village simpleton told the ravens, "Fly high over all the world and search for the Mullah's donkey."

The village fakir shook his copper charms and said, "For just a few dinars I could tell you where to look for your donkey."

The village boys climbed the highest trees and shouted from the branches, "We are looking out over all the world to find the Mullah's donkey."

Finally, completely worn and discouraged, the Mullah sat down in his own open gateway. His friends squatted cross-legged on the ground beside him. Fatima came out quietly with glasses of hot tea to comfort him and his friends. And as he sipped his tea through a sugar lump, the Mullah blamed the donkey for making all this trouble. He could not think of words hard enough to describe the little animal. The Mullah was so very tired that he forgot the years his donkey had been his faithful friend.

"That worthless donkey!" stormed the Mullah. "If I should ever see her again, do you know what I would do?"

"What would you do?" asked Jafar the merchant.

"I would sell that donkey for one dinar." Mullah Nasr-ed-Din named a price that would be an insult to any old donkey that was blind, deaf, lame, cross, and toothless.

Abdullah the baker grinned.

"That would be a good bargain for someone," said Mehmet Ali the coppersmith. He laughed at the thought of the Mullah's sound little donkey being sold for a paltry dinar.

Just then there was the familiar clip-clip of small hoofs coming toward them. And there, ridden by Shoja the young son of Abdullah the baker, was the Mullah's donkey.

"Where did you find her?" asked Daryus the carpenter.

"I knew where I'd go if I were a donkey," answered the boy. "So I looked out in the fields and there she was, grazing with the sheep and the goats."

The Mullah was as happy as he had been discouraged a minute ago. First he hugged and kissed his beloved donkey. Then he hugged and kissed Shoja for finding her. Then he kissed the hand of Abdullah, praising him for being the father of such a clever boy. But his jubilant praise of Shoja was interrupted by a tug on his left sleeve and a poke on his right arm.

The Mullah looked to one side and saw Mehmet Ali holding up a dinar. He looked to the other side and saw Daryus with a dinar in his hand.

"I will buy your donkey," the two men said at the same time.

"My donkey is not for sale," said the Mullah, astonished that anyone should dream of such a thing. "If it were for sale, the price would be many times your dinars."

"But you said that you would sell it for a dinar if you ever found it," Mehmet Ali reminded him. And all the neighbors joined Mehmet Ali in vowing that the Mullah had made exactly that promise.

"I was joking!" The Mullah giggled nervously.

"It did not sound like a joke when you said it," said Daryus who would do anything to make a good bargain. "You were not laughing then."

"But this is not the day for the donkey bazaar in our village." The Mullah was playing for time. He must think of a way to save the donkey and his honor at the same time. It must never be said that the Mullah failed to keep a promise, but surely he would not sell his good donkey for any price, let alone a dinar. He stroked his beard in the way he always did when thinking his hardest. "Meet me at the donkey bazaar on Wednesday. I will sell my donkey for a dinar to the one I think will make the best master."

So till Wednesday the men of the village, and the boys too, were busy being kind to animals whenever the Mullah might be watching. The cats could walk along the ridges of the mud walls with never the fear of a pebble from a slingshot. The dogs were brushed till there was not a tick left to keep them scratching. There were extra shepherd boys going into the fields with the village flocks and herds. Musa's camels had no excuse for their haughty sneering expressions. The scavenging hens had food thrown to them. And the donkeys were treated like kings.

Till Wednesday the Mullah was thinking of a plan whereby he could keep his promise and not lose his donkey. On Tuesday, just before the merchants were pulling down the shutters of their shops for the night, the Mullah bought a piece of rope. For once he did not chat with the salesman about his reasons for buying it.

On Wednesday the donkey bazaar was crowded with men and boys who hoped to be chosen as the perfect master for the dinar's worth of donkey. Over their loud talk they heard a sound that was not always heard in the donkey market. Mixed with the braying of the donkeys there was a sharp and constant "Prrr-t, mee-e-ow! Prrr-t, mee-e-ow!" The voice of a cat was not strange in a land where cats stepped daintily along the top of every mud wall. But this was the voice of a cat who felt out of place and quite uncomfortable.

The men followed the prrr-t mee-e-ow, and there was a cat with a rope around its neck. The other end

of the rope was tied to the tail of the Mullah's donkey. Beside them stood the Mullah smiling happily.

"Yes, my donkey is for sale for just one dinar," the Mullah assured the would-be buyers. "But my donkey and my cat are such good friends that it would be cruel to separate them. Who buys my donkey must buy my cat also."

"And how much is your cat?" asked many voices as men reached in their money bags for another dinar or two.

"Oh, my cat is a very valuable animal. Her great-grandfather lived in the Shah's palace." The Mullah's voice seemed to have a purr in it. "Her price is one hundred dinars."

The men laughed and were glad. After all, everyone knew that the Mullah and his donkey should never be separated.

THE CANARY THAT LIKED
APRICOTS

ONCE Mullah Nasr-ed-Din was riding his white donkey past the fruit orchard of his good friend Mustapha, the best farmer of the whole village. Over the mud walls that surrounded the trees he could see the branches of the apricot tree dotted with ripe golden fruit.

"That reminds me," said the Mullah though there was nobody but his donkey to listen to him. "Mustapha promised to give me some apricots. I can save him the trouble of picking them and bringing them to our house."

The gate was closed but the wall was not too high to be scaled by a man standing on his donkey's saddle. In a whirl of fluttering robes, the Mullah was over the wall and up in the apricot tree. He began sampling the juicy sweet fruit before he noticed that Mustapha's gardener was at work under a nearby

tree. Unfortunately it was a new gardener from another village, a stranger. To him the white turban
and flowing coat of Mullah Nasr-ed-Din meant
nothing at all. Close by stood the gardener's large
dog who obviously did not like strangers.

"What are you doing?" shouted the gardener.
"Don't you know that those are Agha Mustapha's
apricots? What right have you in that tree?"

"Gr-r-r-r!" growled the big dog showing sharp
white fangs.

Now if the Mullah had been most people, he would
have said simply, "My friend Mustapha told me I
could have some of his apricots." But the Mullah
was not most people. Looking down at the gardener,
he thought him a stupid man who might not believe a simple truth. Looking down at the growling
dog, he was sure he would need a very fancy story to
calm him. The Mullah stroked his beard and hunted
for a quick but exciting explanation of why he was
in the tree. A chirp and a warble coming from a
nearby pomegranate tree gave him an idea.

"Don't you know a canary when you see one?"
asked the Mullah. He raised and lowered his arms
in their flowing sleeves, flapping them like wings.
"Who cares if a canary perches in an apricot tree?
Mustapha loves canaries."

The gardener frowned and then he laughed. The dog growled and then he barked.

"If you are a canary, sing to me," the gardener dared the Mullah.

"Gr-r-r-r! Ar-r-r-rf!" rumbled the dog.

"I'll gladly sing for you." Then the Mullah sang in a voice that he tried to make sound like a canary's. Now the Mullah's voice was good when five times a day he gave the call to prayer from the minaret, or when he recited the Koran from the tall pulpit of the mosque on Friday mornings, or when he taught

his boys in the village school. His mullah voice was good, but his canary voice was very bad. He tried to make it high, silvery, and full of trills. But it sounded like nothing in the world but a rather old mullah giving a poor imitation of a canary.

The gardener laughed harder than ever as he said, "I never heard a canary with a voice like yours."

"But do you know every variety of canary?" asked the Mullah. "There are many kinds. A village gardener could not hope to know them all."

"What is your variety?" asked the gardener with a wide grin. He was having such fun that he was forgetting to be cross.

"I belong to the family of canaries famous for . . ." and the Mullah stopped as though he was going to tell of a very special family. "I belong to the family of canaries famous for bad voices."

The gardener laughed again and held his dog by the long hair on the back of its neck. The Mullah finished stuffing his wide belt with apricots. Then he swung from a low branch to the top of the wall, dropped on his donkey's back, and jogged away, singing in time to the clip-clip of his donkey's hoofs. And he sang as the most famous member of the family of canaries famous for bad voices.

BREAD — FREE

ONCE Mullah Nasr-ed-Din's wife said to him, "Our bread is finished. I have no time to bake this morning. I must go to the ditch outside the village to wash our clothes."

The Mullah, kindest of husbands, did not scold his wife for failing to bake bread. He did not talk about how busy he was as the only priest and teacher and judge of the village. Instead he offered, "Let me go to the baker to buy some." His wife agreed. Neither of them thought for a minute of eating a single meal without bread.

The Mullah slipped his wife's woven reed basket over his arm. He glanced at his small white donkey, hobbled beside a pile of straw which one of the hens was using for a nest. No, the bakery was just around the corner. He would go afoot. He felt in his money bag tucked inside his broad belt of gaily figured

65

cloth. He pulled open the heavy street gate and sauntered out into the street.

"I will be back soon," he promised.

One look at the baker's shop, however, told him that his errand might take longer than he had planned. Apparently every other wife in the village had been too busy to bake bread. Some had sent their children. A few had sent their husbands. And many had come themselves. There was such a crowd that the Mullah could not see the top of the head of Abdullah the baker. He could not see the loaves of bread he knew were piled in front of Abdullah. Only his nose told him there was fresh bread warm and fragrant from the oven.

The Mullah counted the people in the crowd, and wondered if there would be any bread left when his turn came. He thought of elbowing his way to the front, but remembered how easy it was for small boys in a crowd to catch hold of his long coat. He must think of a way to buy bread quickly, without standing in the hot sun waiting while the best loaves were chosen by others.

Then the Mullah had an idea. It seemed a good idea to him at the time. He forgot once more how he fell into trouble whenever he tried to play tricks by saying something that was not the truth. He joined the crowd around the bakery door, smiling to think of the fun he was about to have.

"Salam!" he greeted his neighbors.

"Salam!" they returned his greetings.

"I have some news for you," said the Mullah in a voice so low that everyone crowded closer to listen. "Have you heard about the party at the big house of Agha Abdul Karim, the rich rug merchant?"

"No," they all answered. "What sort of party?"

"Haven't you heard that he is giving a loaf of bread — free — to everyone who comes to his house?" asked the Mullah. He saw the excitement running through the crowd.

"When?" came from behind a woman's chaddur.

"I advise you all to hurry," said the Mullah. "You would not want to be late."

Like a flock of sheep following a new leader, the crowd left the bakery and ran in the direction of the big house of Agha Abdul Karim. There were sharp voices as they got in each others' way in the narrow alley between the walls. There was the pounding of many feet as more people joined, believing that where so many were going it must be good to follow.

Alone at the bakery, Mullah Nasr-ed-Din stood

and smiled. Leisurely he stepped inside the little shop. He saw the big white-washed clay oven with its fire of twigs and brush burned down to a glowing smudge. He saw the round loaves and the long loaves of bread, fresh from the oven. He saw the flat crisp loaves that had been baked under sizzling stones. He could take his pick. He took the money bag from his belt to see if he had dinars enough to buy both a round loaf and a flat loaf.

As he looked at his money, he began to wonder why

he should spend it. He thought of all his neighbors, running to the big house of Agha Abdul Karim to get a free loaf of bread. Why should he buy it when every other person in the village was getting it free? He stroked his beard and thought.

"Which loaf will you take?" Abdullah had the right to feel impatient with the man who had dispersed his crowd of customers. He seemed in a hurry to lay his hands on the Mullah's money.

"I want none of your bread!" answered the Mullah. "Why should I be the only man in the village to pay good dinars for bread today?"

He tucked his money bag within his broad cotton belt. He picked up his coat, the better to run. His soft old slippers with their pointed-up toes and their folded-back heels scattered pebbles behind them, so fast did he disappear up the street that led to the house of Agha Abdul Karim. He must hurry before all that delicious free bread was given away.

As he neared the walled garden of the big house of Agha Abdul Karim, he sniffed for the good smell of freshly baked bread. Only the sweetness of jasmine blossoms filled his nose. He was almost there and quite out of breath from running when he met the first of his neighbors coming back. They were clumping along slowly, looking quite disgusted about something.

"Where are you hurrying, Mullah?" asked the young cobbler Ahmad.

"To the house of Agha Abdul Karim," the Mullah called back as he ran past them, his coat blowing straight out behind him.

"Why?" asked Mehmet Ali the coppersmith.

"For a free loaf of bread!" floated back on the breeze which he made as he ran.

"But that was just one of your jokes!" many voices shouted after him. "And a poor joke at that," added the loud voice of Daryus.

The Mullah was so far away that his neighbors could scarcely hear his answer, "Who knows? There might be something in the rumor after all!"

THE VOICE FROM THE
MINARET

ALWAYS Mullah Nasr-ed-Din was happy to climb
the spiral staircase to the little roofed balcony that
ringed the top of the small minaret of his village
mosque. Always he liked the sound of his own voice
calling the villagers to kneel in prayer, touching fore-
heads to the ground wherever they were — at sun-
rise, at midday, at sunset.

One day, when Mullah Nasr-ed-Din gave the call
to prayer from the minaret, he was more than usually
pleased with the music of his voice. As he chanted,
he gazed out over the rounded mud roofs of the
village homes, over the wheat and cotton fields that
surrounded the village, over the barren plain that
spread in all directions beyond the irrigated fields.
He saw the gray mountains that rose in a huge circle
at the edges of the plain. He thought of the plateaus
beyond the mountains. He smiled as he chanted,

thinking of his voice carrying on and on in ever-widening waves of sound. The more he thought of this, the louder he chanted:

> *"There is no god but Allah*
> *And Mohammed is his prophet."*

The minute he had called the last note, he ran down the minaret's curving stairway, two steps at a time. Reaching the bottom step, he slipped his feet into his worn shoes with their up-pointing toes and

their down-folded heels. He ran out the minaret door without stopping to close it. His long coat blew straight behind him as he ran through the village. He headed out into the open country of irrigated fields, barren plain, high mountains and plateaus beyond them. He must find the answer to the question that had come to him in the minaret. He ran so fast that farmers leaned on their hoes to watch him. Children playing in the water ditches stopped their splashing to shout after him. Women dropped their veils the better to stare at him. A train of loaded camels looked disdainfully down their proud noses at him. Sheep grazing near the road ran away in fright, their fat tails bobbing. A family riding side by side on donkeyback made a single file to let him pass.

"Where are you going in such a hurry?" called the father of the riding family. But the Mullah ran so fast that his answer was swallowed by the wind before it could be heard.

As the Mullah ran he met Mustapha riding his horse from work in his own apricot orchard. The farmer turned his horse and rode along beside the Mullah.

"Where are you hurrying?" asked Mustapha.

"My voice — from the minaret — was very good today," panted the Mullah.

"Of course," his friend agreed good-naturedly. "But where are you going now in such a rush?"

And the Mullah answered without slowing his pace, "I am running — to find out — how far — my voice — carried!"

THE CROW AND THE SOAP

ONE day Fatima, the wife of Mullah Nasr-ed-Din,
went to wash her clothes in the ditch that brought
water to the village. She carried a flat stick to pound
them clean. Because she was very lucky that day, she
carried also a small piece of yellow soap to rub on
them. This soap was very precious. It was expensive
if she bought it in the market, and it was hard to make
if she saved fat to boil in the big kettle in her yard.
But what a difference it made as she pounded with
her flat stick to get the clothes clean in the cool flowing water of the ditch.

Usually there were other women washing their
clothes. Today Fatima happened to be alone except
for a big black crow that perched in the branches of
a willow tree and greeted her with an angry "Caw,
caw, caw!" Fatima would have liked to have women
to gossip with her. On the other hand, had they been
there they would have asked to share her precious

soap. The Mullah had brought it to her as a special surprise just yesterday when he had sold his figs for a good price. She must make it last as long as possible.

"Caw, caw, caw!" scolded the big black crow.

Slap — slap — slap went Fatima's stick as she pounded her clothes in the flowing water. She paid no attention to the crow in the willow tree.

Suddenly the big black bird swooped toward her. Fatima threw up her hands to shield her face. But it was not the woman that interested the crow. With

his sharp beak he picked up the piece of soap. He flapped his ragged black wings and flew to the top-most branch of the willow tree.

"My soap!" screamed Fatima. And a very good voice she had for screaming. "My soap! My soap! Fly back here with my soap!"

Fatima's voice was so shrill and so loud that it was heard easily in the village. The Mullah, talking with his friends Jafar and Mehmet Ali near the gate of the village walls, recognized it. His good wife must be in great danger! He went running to rescue her, his long coat fluttering behind him as he ran.

"What is the matter?" he called. "I will save you, my Fatima. What has happened?"

"My soap! My soap!" Fatima's scream was near enough to him now that he could understand her words.

"What about your soap?" He stood beside her, wondering how a mere piece of yellow soap could have given her such terrible pain.

"It is gone," sobbed Fatima. "A big crow grabbed it in his horrid beak and flew away with it. Ah wahi! Ah wahi! It was the very best soap. It was the very piece of soap you gave me yesterday. When can I ever have another?"

At first the Mullah felt almost as badly as Fatima did about the stolen soap. He knew how much he had paid for it in the bazaar only the day before in spite of his best bargaining. Gazing upward, he could see the black of the crow's feathers in the topmost branches of the willow tree. Suddenly he realized that everything had happened for the best after all.

"There, there!" the Mullah soothed his screaming wife. "Did you notice the color of the crow's coat?"

"Black of course!" Fatima stopped crying to wonder why her husband should ask such a simple question.

"Yes, blacker than the dirtiest of our clothes," said Mullah Nasr-ed-Din. "He needs the soap much more than we do. Let him keep it!"

THE QUIVERING NEEDLE

ONCE Mullah Nasr-ed-Din was walking through the great covered bazaar of Isfahan. He bowed to right and to left as he recognized friends buying, selling, or merely bargaining. He loved the excitement of the bazaar where he could always meet someone just back from a journey. From Tabriz or Hamadan. Possibly from faraway India or Egypt.

Where two of the covered streets of the bazaar met, he found a group of men with their heads close together over something held in the hand of a camel driver named Musa. As the Mullah naturally wished to know what was going on, his turbaned head was soon in the huddle.

"Salam," the men greeted him.

"Salam," the Mullah replied.

"We were wondering what this strange thing is," one of the men told the Mullah. "When Musa was riding his camel across the desert, he saw it shining on the ground."

"I climbed down from my camel," Musa took up the story, "and picked it up. But I do not know what it is. I thought that some of the wise men in the bazaar could tell me what it is. But nobody can guess."

"You know everything, Mullah." It was Mustapha speaking. He had ridden to the city to sell his apricots. "Can you tell us what it is?"

Mullah Nasr-ed-Din stared at the small round box of metal and glass in the palm of Musa's sun-browned hand. Inside the box he saw letters and a tiny needle. It was this needle that was most strange. It quivered as the box was turned, but it always came to rest pointing in the same direction. Mullah Nasr-ed-Din took the little box in his hand. He turned it this way and that way. The needle quivered, but always it pointed north. The Mullah stroked his beard in the way he did when he was thinking his hardest. Then he handed the little box back to Musa.

"What is it?" the camel driver asked. The men waited hopefully for the answer. They expected wise and knowing words from the learned Mullah. They were all most curious about the quivering needle that had a magic way of always pointing north no matter how much it was twisted and turned.

For a moment the Mullah stroked his beard and said nothing. Then he did a most amazing thing. First he cried. Then he laughed. He repeated this as long as the men could stand watching him — crying and laughing, laughing and crying, crying and laughing.

"Why are you crying?" asked some of the men.

"Why are you laughing?" asked others.

"Nobody, not even a mullah, should cry and laugh at the same time," said Mustapha.

"I'll tell you why I am crying and why I am laughing," promised the Mullah. By this time every man and boy in that part of the great covered bazaar was crowding close to the Mullah to hear what wise thing he would say. Those who did not know the Mullah were being told about him by those who did. Women, drawing their chuddars over their faces, made up errands to keep them in that part of the bazaar.

"I am crying," began the Mullah, "because not one of you is smart enough to name this little round box with its quivering needle. How very stupid of you all! I am ashamed for you. Do you wonder that

I cry?" The Mullah looked from man to man. They withered under his scorn for their ignorance. Even the boys squirmed and drooped in their shame at knowing so little. The women sighed under their chuddars, glad they were not expected to know very much beyond the care of their houses and children. They did not wonder that the learned Mullah was ashamed that the people of the great city of Isfahan were so stupid.

Mustapha, who knew the Mullah better than the others did, was brave enough to change the subject. "You have told us why you are crying," he said. "Now, good Mullah, will you tell us why you are laughing?"

And the Mullah laughed as he made answer, "I am laughing because I also do not know what it is!"

THE DONKEY'S TAIL

ONCE Mullah Nasr-ed-Din opened his street gate to let in his neighbor Hosen whose shoulders were stooped from his work. He took care of the underground canals and the open ditches that brought the village water from the mountains.

"Salam!" the men greeted one another.

"Why are you barefoot today?" the Mullah asked.

"Because I have lost my shoes," answered Hosen, rubbing the spots where the pebbles had bruised them.

"Tell me what happened," invited the Mullah.

That was exactly what Hosen planned to do, so the two men sat together under the big mulberry tree while he told the story of his lost shoes.

"Yesterday I went to drink tea at the house of Hajji Mahdi," began Hosen in his meek low voice. "There were ten of us there. Of course we left our shoes at the door when we went in. I was the last to arrive. I saw the nine pairs of shoes lined up outside the door, none so new as mine. I left my shoes with the others and went in the house. We talked — and drank tea — and talked — and drank tea.

The Mullah stroked his beard and nodded to show that he was listening. He was used to hearing the troubles of all his village neighbors. That was part of his duty as teacher-priest-judge for the village.

"One by one the men went home," Hosen drawled. "I was the last one to leave. And when I looked outside the door, what did I see?"

Glancing at Hosen's bare feet, the Mullah guessed. "You saw that your shoes were gone."

"Exactly!" Hosen thought it was a good omen that the Mullah could answer that first question so well. Then he asked a harder one, "Where were my shoes?"

"One of the nine men carried them away," answered the Mullah. "One of them is playing a trick on you."

"True," agreed Hosen, cheered that the Mullah understood so well. "But which one?"

"That is what we must learn," said the Mullah. The two men sat quietly while the Mullah thought. Fatima brought glasses of hot sweet tea to help in the thinking. At last he had his idea. "Tell all nine men to come to my house tomorrow morning together. I will put them through a test that will show without fail which one took your shoes."

Early next morning the Mullah was very busy. First he was down on his knees picking something in his garden. Then he went into the donkey's stable. Coming out, he called Fatima to pour water over his hands from the slim-spouted copper pitcher. By the time the men arrived, he was sitting cross-legged in the doorway of his home, appearing every inch the village judge that he was.

After the salams of greeting were over, he said, "I understand that one of you men took Hosen's shoes while he drank tea with Hajji Mahdi." Each man put on his best not-me expression. The Mullah went on, "It would save trouble if one of you would give the shoes back to Hosen now." The men eyed one another with a you-do-it expression, but none had a word to say.

"It will be easy to find who took the shoes." The Mullah stroked his beard and glanced from one face to another to see who seemed worried. "I want you all to go, one at a time, into my donkey's stable. Each one of you must close the door behind him. Then he must take hold of the tufted end of my donkey's tail and pull it — gently, of course. When the thief pulls the tail, my donkey will bray."

The men did as the Mullah ordered. One by one they went into the stable. Each one closed the door a minute or two, then opened it and came out. Not once did the little white donkey bray.

"Your test did not work," sighed Hosen, very much disappointed. He had been so sure the wise Mullah could help.

"My test has just begun," announced the Mullah. "I want you men to pass by me, one by one. And as you pass, I want each one of you to touch my nose and my beard — first with the right hand and then with the left."

The men filed past the Mullah. Each one touched the Mullah's nose and beard — first with the right hand and then with the left. Ahmad, whose school days under the Mullah were not long ago, could not resist the chance to give the nose a little tweak and the beard a little pull. Hosen watched with little hope. He feared that this second test was no better than the first. The last man passed before the Mullah spoke.

"Daryus!" He pointed an accusing finger. "*You* took the shoes. You have hidden them. Give them back to Hosen."

"It was just a joke," mumbled Daryus, red-faced. "They are in my donkey's saddlebag, by your gate. But how did you guess?"

"That was easy!" The Mullah could laugh now. "Smell your hands."

Daryus sniffed and found nothing more than the usual smells of his donkey, saddle leather, carpenter's tools, and the last food he ate.

"Now smell the hands of any of the other men," the Mullah chuckled.

Daryus smelled as the men held out their hands to him. "Spearmint!" he said. "They all smell of the spearmint that grows in your garden."

Just then there was a friendly bray and the donkey came trotting out of the stable. She felt she had been alone long enough.

"Smell my donkey's tail," the Mullah ordered Daryus. "Smell the tufted end of the tail that you alone were afraid to pull for fear she would bray that you were the thief."

Daryus caught the end of the donkey's flicking tail and held it to his nose. "Spearmint! It smells of spearmint!" Now he understood the Mullah's test. And because it was such a very good test, Daryus found himself laughing with the other men as he went out to his donkey's saddlebags for Hosen's shoes.

THE STONE IN THE GARDEN

As THE years went on, the beard of Mullah Nasr-ed-Din changed from black to gray, then from gray to white. Less and less of a fringe of hair showed when he took off his heavy white turban to fan himself on hottest days. He spent more and more time dozing under the big mulberry tree in his walled garden. Nowadays he asked his donkey to come to a full halt before he climbed off her back. And when he read from the Koran, he noticed that the words sometimes looked blurred.

But woe to anyone who made the mistake of calling the Mullah an old man! He was still the center of village life, and well he knew it. He taught the boys to read from the Koran. He gave wise judgments in every village quarrel. He climbed the tall pulpit in the mosque every Friday to preach and pray and read from the Holy Koran. He climbed the still taller spiral staircase of the minaret five times a day to chant:

> *"There is no god but Allah*
> *And Mohammed is his prophet."*

He was a good neighbor to everyone in the village. He still tended his garden of cucumbers and other vegetables behind his own mud walls.

Ahmad should have known all this. He should never have made the mistake that nearly threw the Mullah into the worst rage the village had ever seen. But the Mullah had appeared old when Ahmad was a boy in the village school. He had seemed older as Ahmad grew from a cobbler's apprentice to a cobbler with a shop of his own.

It happened one morning in the wheat bazaar.

"Let me help you, Mullah Nasr-ed-Din," offered Ahmad. The white-bearded man who had taught him to read some ten years ago was stooped under the bag of wheat he was carrying. Ahmad took the load from the Mullah's back, hoisted it easily to his own wide shoulders, and led the way to the Mullah's donkey. The Mullah, frowning and muttering, scuffed hurriedly behind the long stride of the young man who had so recently been his pupil.

"This is too heavy a load for an old man to carry," Ahmad scolded gently. He swung the bag from his shoulder into one of the saddlebags of the Mullah's donkey. "It's time you let the younger men do the hard work."

"Old man!" shouted Mullah Nasr-ed-Din. "Who says I'm old?"

"Not old of course," Ahmad tried to soothe him. "I meant you are not as strong as when you were younger."

"I'm just as strong now as I ever was. I'm as strong as I was when I was your age — or Riza's age." The Mullah pointed at the thirteen-year-old apprentice of the potter. "I was never stronger in my life than I am this minute!"

"Yes, yes, of course," agreed Ahmad. But his voice did not sound as though he believed his words.

"Yes, yes, of course," echoed the men and boys who had come running at the Mullah's shout.

The Mullah looked from one to the other. He was no fool. He could read on every face that the polite words were hiding the belief that the Mullah was losing his strength as his hair fell out and his beard turned white. He did not like that.

"I'll prove to you that I am as strong today as when

I was young," stormed the Mullah. He did hope he
could think fast and find a way to prove his strength.

"Prove it to us!" The men sat cross-legged on the
hard ground of the market place. The proof might
take a long time. They meant to be comfortable while
waiting. The Mullah paced up and down before
them, searching for a way to prove that his strength
was not failing. Ah, he had it. He sat down cross-
legged on the ground, the better to talk with his
neighbors.

"When I was a boy," he began, "there was a big

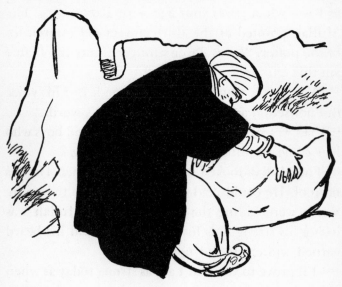

stone in the garden of my father's home. I used to test my strength by trying to lift it. Whenever I felt that I had grown bigger and stronger, I would tug and tug to raise that stone. But I could not lift it. I tried when I was the age of Riza here, but I could not move it. The last thing I did when I left my father's home to go to the school for mullahs was to try to lift that stone, but I could not budge it. When I came back as a mullah, the age of Ahmad here, I tried again. I strained and I heaved and I hoisted, but I could not stir it by so much as a hair's breadth. Well, just the other day . . ."

The Mullah paused and the men drew closer to listen. They could feel important words coming. The Mullah went on, "Just the other day I was in the old neighborhood where I lived as a boy. The old house had crumbled and the walls had not been kept repaired. I walked into the old garden and sat down to rest. There I saw the stone on which I had tested my strength as I grew from childhood to manhood. I remembered that I could never move that stone when I was young. I wanted to test the strength I have in my arms and back today. I stooped and took hold of it with both hands — old man that I am . . ."

Closer still crowded the men as the Mullah's voice grew lower and more impressive. His last words were only a whisper, but every man in the crowd heard them, "And I cannot move the stone now."

THE BABY MOSQUE

MULLAH NASR-ED-DIN was wise to help other folks when they were in trouble. But he was not always wise when he was in trouble himself. Once he was telling his merchant friend Jafar about one of his worries.

"Sometimes I am not a patient teacher for the village boys," he said, stroking his beard thoughtfully. "I scold them when they are slow to memorize the words of the Holy Koran. I forget that boys would rather play than study."

"Oh, Mullah," Jafar reminded him, "if one of us does wrong, you tell us to ask Allah to make us good. Do you forget to ask Allah to make you patient?"

"You are right, Jafar," agreed Mullah Nasr-ed-Din.

"It is not enough to talk to Allah about this worry of yours in our little village mosque with its dome and minarets made of common mud bricks," Jafar advised him. "Carry your best prayer rug to the great mosque in Isfahan, the Shah's mosque with its tall minarets and its dome of lapis lazuli, turquoise and gold. Make your preparations for prayer, washing three times in the water of the beautiful fountain in the court of the mosque. Lay your prayer rug in the most beautiful prayer niche with its mosaic work in blue and white tile. Then bow before Allah and ask his help. Surely he will hear what you say in that great and famous mosque."

That seemed a good idea to Mullah Nasr-ed-Din. The next day he threw one leg over his donkey's back, adjusted his long flowing robes for comfortable riding, and jogged along the dusty road to Isfahan. As other travelers joined him, he sat as he so often sat, facing the donkey's tail, the better to talk with the men behind him. He passed the small mosques and the old brick-domed mosque. He rode straight to the great mosque of the Shah facing the beautiful square in the center of Isfahan.

Telling his donkey to wait for him, he went inside. He washed three times in the flowing fountain. He chose the most beautiful prayer niche of blue and white mosaics, spread his best prayer rug in it, and prayed in the singing words of the Koran:

"To Allah belongs every one dwelling in the heavens
and the earth,
that He may requite all those who have done evil
and requite all those who have done good."

He felt awed by the great dome over his head. He felt
shabby among the well-dressed men who came to
pray in the mosque of the Shah. It was hard to keep
his mind on the prayers he would recite from the
Holy Koran. It was harder still to think of any words
of his own to ask Allah's help. There was so much
going on about him. But on and on he prayed, very
sure that prayers said in such a beautiful mosque
would fly fast to Allah even if the one who prayed
did sometimes forget what words he was saying.

Next day, when he met his class of mischievous
boys, he expected to be the most patient and under-
standing teacher of all Persia. To his great disap-
pointment, he lost his temper before the boys had
been with him one short hour. His trip to the great
mosque of the Shah had been wasted.

That evening he went earlier than usual to the
little mud-brick mosque of his own village. He looked
around at its plain walls with no prayer niche of blue
and white mosaic tiles. Mullah Nasr-ed-Din did not

have even his old prayer rug to unroll and lay on the floor, its design pointing toward Mecca. But he felt like talking to Allah, asking help to be a patient teacher for boys who would rather play than study.

So Mullah Nasr-ed-Din knelt on the hard-packed clay of the little village mosque and talked with Allah about all the things that bothered him. Then he climbed the minaret to call the people of the village to evening prayer.

The next day he met his boys with a joke, a smile, and a pat on the shoulder. He felt like a good and patient teacher again. The boys studied as they had not worked in weeks. His prayers in the little mosque had been answered!

As soon as school was over, the Mullah did a strange thing. He saddled his little donkey, threw one long leg over its back, and jogged out of the village between waving fields of wheat to the city and its great mosque of the Shah. Leaving his donkey, he walked boldly into the big mosque. He stood under its dome of lapis lazuli, turquoise and gold. He was careful to stand in the spot of echoes so that what he had to say would be repeated again and again under the great dome.

"You great big mosque," intoned the Mullah in

a loud voice that echoed and re-echoed under the vaulted ceiling. "You should be ashamed of yourself. You could not do what your baby mosque was able to do. You should come to our village and take lessons from the little mosque."

HIDING IN THE WELL

FATIMA could not sleep so soundly as did her good husband Mullah Nasr-ed-Din. He could snore pleasantly through a cat-fight on the garden wall, or the baying of a neighbor's restless dog, or the tapping cane of the village night watchman. He could sleep even through the braying of a donkey having a bad dream. Not so Fatima! The least noise outside the window would have her sitting up in bed. Two noises under the window would have her poking her sleeping husband, "Wake up and protect me!"

One moonlit night in the cool of winter, Fatima thought she heard the muffled step-step of thieves in the garden. She poked the Mullah. He grunted and slept on. She heard sounds again. This time her poke was so vigorous that the Mullah sat up in bed.

"What's the matter?" he yawned.

"Listen!" she demanded.

He stumbled across the room and stuck his head

out the window into a world bathed in moonlight. But he could hear nothing but the usual night noises.

"They may have stopped walking around now," Fatima admitted. "But I won't sleep another wink till you go out in the yard and see if anyone is there."

The Mullah knew that Fatima meant what she said. Moreover, he knew that he would not sleep either till he satisfied her. So out into the yard he stumbled. He felt her watching from the window to be sure that he peered into every cranny where a thief might possibly be hiding. He poked behind trees. One of his hens squawked dreamily from her perch in a low branch. He wakened his sleepy donkey by prying into every corner of her shed. "Hee-haw!" she complained in a yawning bray. He walked around the house twice. Everything was as it should be. He started into the house, but he heard a whisper from the window where Fatima stood.

"You have not looked in the well," came in her loud whisper.

"No fool would hide in the well," was the Mullah's disgusted answer.

"Look in the well," commanded Fatima.

Ordinarily he would argue with anyone, even his wife. But tonight he was too sleepy for an argument.

He knew that the quickest way back to sleep was to do whatever his wife asked.

He dragged his feet over to the well and flopped down to his hands and knees. The moon was so bright that he could look easily into the depths of the well. Suddenly he was wide awake. Looking up at him from the water was a man just about his age and just about as bald as he was.

"A good place for you, you old idiot!" The Mullah's voice made hollow echoes as he called down the well. "There's no harm you can do hiding in the

well. I'm not going to pull you out now. You can stay there till morning, you cowardly thief!"

So the Mullah went back to bed. Just before he rolled off to sleep, he told Fatima about the thief hiding in the well.

"Are you sure he can't climb out?" asked Fatima.

"Very sure," drawled the Mullah, half asleep already.

"I want to take a look at him. Will you come with me?" she asked. But the Mullah was already snoring.

She hated going into the garden alone, but she had the Mullah's word that the thief could not crawl out of the well. With her own eyes she had watched her husband search every other nook of the yard for prowlers.

She stepped silently out into the moonlight. She walked noiselessly across the yard to the well. Without a sound she fell to hands and knees to peek into the well.

There was no man to be seen down there. He must be hiding somewhere in the shadows of the well. But what she did see filled her with shocked amazement. Peering up at her with a face full of surprise was a round-eyed woman just about Fatima's own age.

"Puh, puh, puh!" Fatima was disgusted that any woman should be so bold as to take part in a night-time robbery. She hurried back to tell her husband the disgraceful news.

"It is a shame!" she sputtered angrily. "What bold people! It is not enough for that thief to hide in our well! He brings his wife with him!"

name, howling it in time to their marching. Other men and boys appeared from the shadows, following the noise to find out what it was all about.

The ruffians were wailing their loudest when they knocked at the Mullah's street gate. They softened their wails to low moans as they waited for the answer. Curious men and boys made a silent circle behind them.

"Open the gate, please," they heard the Mullah call to one of his friends. The boys moaned louder as the door creaked open.

"Bring a light, Fatima," they heard the Mullah call to his wife. They groaned and wailed the name of the dead donkey.

"Who in the world can it be?" they heard Fatima ask her husband.

Then the loud voice of the Mullah carried easily across the walls to the boys in the street and to the men who were watching them. "It must be the brothers of the donkey. His family has come to mourn for him."

Then the boys sneaked off into the darkness. On all sides they heard laughing voices repeating, "The brothers of the donkey! The brothers of the donkey!"

TWO COWS

IF ANY boy in the village wanted to learn to read, it was the Mullah's duty to teach him. Sometimes a large class met in the small mud hut in the yard of the village mosque. Sometimes there was no class at all.

Once Mullah Nasr-ed-Din was teaching a class of ten boys, all sitting cross-legged on the hard clay floor. Their one book was the Koran in Arabic. They sat there on a drowsy spring morning reading the same words over and over. Each was reading a different selection from the Koran. Each was reading in his loudest voice to show how hard he was studying. While Shoja was chanting:

"To Allah belongs the East, and the West.
Wheresoever you turn yourselves, there is the face
of Allah,"

Mahmoud was droning,

"Glory to Allah in the evening and the morning:
Praise be to Him in the heavens and the earth
at night and through the noonday,"

and Sohrab's singsong voice was asking

"Have you not seen how Allah drives on the clouds
then marshals them together,
then turns them into masses?"

And so it went — ten selections from the Koran being memorized by ten boys with loud and monotonous voices.

The steady murmur was like a lullaby to Mullah Nasr-ed-Din. When a fly would light on his nose or a raven would caw outside the window, he would rouse with a start. He would wonder if the boys were as sleepy as he was, and would think of some way of testing them. Sometimes he would ask questions about what they were studying. Sometimes he would ask the first question that popped into his head.

On this particular morning, he was roused by the clank of the bells of cows passing in the street. Naturally, the first question that came to his mind was about cows, rather than about the Koran.

"Boys!" boomed the Mullah in a voice to wake himself as well as his boy pupils. Those who were studying dropped their books. Those who had been dozing picked theirs up. All stared at the Mullah.

"I have a question to ask you," he began. The boys all sat at attention, listening.

"Suppose two cows are walking along a narrow street. One cow is leading. The other cow is close behind. The second cow wishes to be leader. She tries to pass. The first cow moves to block her way. There is confusion of switching tails and tossing horns. There is a bellow of pain from the first cow. The sharp horns of the second cow have pierced the thick skin of the first cow." The Mullah paused, stroked his beard, and asked, "Do you all follow exactly what has happened to the two cows?"

"We do," chorused the boys, all wide awake now.

"Are you ready for the question?" asked the Mullah.

"We are ready," the boys answered as though they had one voice instead of ten voices.

"Then this is the question." The Mullah pointed at boy after boy to be sure they were all listening. "Which cow can say, 'I have tail and horns at the same end of my body'?"

"The first cow," guessed Rustam quickly while the other boys agreed.

"No!" The Mullah clicked his tongue and uptilted his head in the Persian way of saying "No!"

"The second cow," said Mahmoud. The boys murmured agreement.

"No!" The Mullah clicked his tongue again.

"Both cows," guessed Sohrab. The other boys repeated the same answer which seemed to be the only possible one left for them. "Both cows."

"No!" was the answer once more.

The boys scratched their heads and tried to think

what the answer could be. Not the first cow. Not the second cow. Not both cows. They asked the Mullah to repeat the question again.

Slowly the Mullah described again the two cows fighting for first place in a narrow street. He told of the horns of the second cow sticking into the rump of the first cow. Then he repeated the question, "Which cow can say, 'I have both tail and horns at the same end of my body'?"

"The first cow," Jamshid guessed in a small uncertain voice.

"The second cow," guessed Sohrab because someone must guess something.

"Both cows," guessed Parviz half-heartedly.

But to each the Mullah answered "No" and clicked his tongue to make it perfectly sure that he meant "No."

The boys looked helplessly at one another, and found each face as blank as the next. "We give up. You must tell us the answer."

"Neither cow could say it," grinned Mullah Nasr-ed-Din. "You boys have forgotten that cows cannot talk!"

ONE! TWO! THREE!

THERE was pounding on the street gate of Mullah Nasr-ed-Din's home. It was not the gentle knock of a person coming for a chat and a glass of tea. It was the hurried banging of someone in trouble.

The pounding disturbed the Mullah's afternoon nap in the shade of the mulberry tree in his walled garden. He sat up and rubbed his eyes. He straightened his white turban that had fallen over one eye as he slept. He put his arms into the long coat with its flowing sleeves. He slipped his feet into his worn shoes with their turned-up toes and their folded-down heels.

By this time his wife had opened the street gate. A stream of excited villagers poured into the Mullah's garden.

"Daoud is in trouble," was all that the Mullah could learn from the jumble of their chatter.

"What has happened to Daoud?" The Mullah

spoke calmly to quiet them. His long experience as priest, teacher and judge had taught him that people could not tell a straight story when they were too stirred up. "Just one of you tell me. Jafar, you talk."

"You know that Daoud is building a house for himself," began Jafar the merchant.

"I know," agreed the Mullah. "Yesterday it was all done except for putting matting and clay on the rafters of the roof."

"Today men were helping him finish," went on Jafar. "He climbed the stairs to the roof. Then they threw wet mud up to him. Beginning by the stairs, he smoothed the mud. Now he has a beautiful roof of soft clay that will be perfect when it hardens. But Daoud is standing in the corner farthest from the stairs. If he walks across the fresh clay to the stairs, there will always be deep footprints on it. What can he do?"

"How about jumping?" asked the Mullah.

"Too high," chorused the people.

"How about his staying up there till it dries?" asked the Mullah.

And the answers were so loud and so many that the Mullah could understand only that the people thought that a very poor idea indeed.

"Let me think." The Mullah stroked his beard and walked up and down gazing at the ground. "Many times I have saved people. Saving someone from a roof should not be too hard. I'm thinking about the method I used to save three men."

The people were calmer now. With the Mullah stroking his beard in his best thinking manner, they felt that Daoud was as good as on the ground already. They even stopped chattering, waiting for the next words of wisdom from their Mullah.

"Bring a rope," the wise words came. "I will meet you and the rope at Daoud's new house. All will be well."

The people drew a deep sigh of relief. Some, knowing that all was well because the Mullah had said so, went back to their work or their naps. Others went to find the rope and carry it to Daoud's house.

Soon the Mullah, rope in hand, was standing with the neighbors below Daoud. That poor fellow was growing hot, hungry, and impatient on his lonely roof perch. He was glad to see the confident smile on the Mullah's face.

"Catch one end of this rope, Daoud!" The Mullah tied one end of the rope about his own waist. He tossed the other to the poor farmer on the roof. The first throw missed, and the second. But Daoud caught the third.

"Tie the rope around your waist," ordered the Mullah. Daoud did as he was told. He tied a hard knot and tested it for strength.

"Now I will count three." The Mullah grasped the rope near the place where it was knotted around his waist. "When I say 'three,' I will pull."

"Are you sure that is the right thing to do?" asked Daoud looking down at the hard ground below him.

"Are you sure?" repeated the watching neighbors.

"Of course I'm sure," answered the Mullah. "I have saved three men in precisely this same way."

Though Daoud knew that the Mullah was very wise, something seemed wrong with the plan. He did not want to question the Mullah's wisdom, but he did wish he could think it over a few minutes. The Mullah, however, never questioned his own plans, and seldom waited for others to question them. He was wasting no time in getting Daoud down from the roof — poor, hot and hungry fellow.

"Ready now," the Mullah called up to Daoud. "One! Two! Three!" And at the "three" the Mullah gave a mighty heave on the rope — so great a heave that the Mullah himself fell backward as Daoud catapulted through the air and landed with a horrid thud on the hard ground.

The Mullah lay on his back waiting for someone to run to his help, but nobody paid any attention to him. Finally, he picked himself up. He found the crowd gathered about Daoud, trying to decide how many of his bones were broken.

"What happened?" they yelled at the Mullah.

"Something went wrong. I don't know what." The Mullah stroked his beard and gazed sadly at the

bruised and battered Daoud. "I did exactly what I have done before when I have saved people. Three times I have saved men by tying ropes around their waists, and counting three, and pulling. Not one of them had so much as a scratch."

"But why was Daoud hurt?" asked the people.

"It must be that his time for breaking bones had come," explained the Mullah. "Kismet. It was fate."

"Kismet. His time had come," murmured the people. Daoud alone was not satisfied.

"Where were those three people when you saved them by tying ropes around their waists, counting three, and pulling?" whispered the tired voice of Daoud.

"They had fallen into wells," answered the Mullah.

HUNTING IN THE LIGHT

THE moon shone through the window into the little house where Mullah Nasr-ed-Din and his wife were getting ready for the night by the light of a single flickering candle. There was the clink of a coin dropping and rolling across the floor.

"Let's wait till morning to hunt for it." The Mullah yawned.

"I won't sleep a wink unless I find it," snapped Fatima, falling to her knees to search. The Mullah knew that if Fatima did not sleep, he would not be allowed to close his eyes either. So down on his knees he creaked to join her in hunting for the lost coin.

"I think it rolled this way," he said, creeping toward the door.

"No, I think it rolled this way," said Fatima, creeping in the opposite direction.

They searched under tables and chairs. They explored every dark corner with only the wavering candle for light. They scraped their knees and bumped their heads. They knocked over a pottery water jug full of water. But Fatima would not give up the hunt.

The Mullah stood up to stretch his cramped back muscles. He glanced through the window at the moonlit world outside. Immediately he ran into the courtyard, dropped on his knees, and started crawling about. He patted the ground searchingly with his hands, first on one side and then on the other.

"What are you doing out there?" It was Fatima's voice from the doorway.

"Looking for the lost coin, of course," said the Mullah as he crept round and round the trunk of the mulberry tree, silvery in the moonlight.

"You lost your coin in the house, Stupid!" his wife reminded him. "We heard it roll along the floor. Remember? Why are you hunting for it outdoors?"

"It's dark in the house. There's no light but that one sputtering candle," explained the Mullah. He crawled through the cucumber patch peering under the big leaves one by one. "It's too dark in the house to find anything. But, thanks to that beautiful moon, it is almost as light as day out here. Who would hunt for anything in that dark house when there is such a wonderful place as this to look for a lost coin?" And the Mullah crawled toward the wall where the jasmine flowers gleamed white and fragrant in the moonlight.

STEAM — HOW MUCH

MULLAH NASR-ED-DIN had finished his bowl of fresh mast at the tea house in his village. He was very comfortable. The grapevine growing on the arbor over his head sheltered him from the beating heat of the sun. The bench, covered with a bright Persian rug, was as pleasant a place for napping as for sipping tea.

"I'll doze just a minute," the Mullah told Masud the tea-house owner. Then he lay down. He threw one flowing sleeve over his face to keep away the flies, and was fast asleep. The voices about him faded off into murmurs that were part of his dreams. The good smell of stew cooking in the open kettle in the yard made a pleasant background for his dreams.

The smell of boiling stew meant more, however, to hungry Abdul Ali who walked slowly by, carrying his loaf of dark bread — his only food. Once more his crops had failed when other farmers were

bringing in their harvests. It was a long time since
he had eaten anything as tasty as that stew with its
generous chunks of meat. Bread, day after day, was
good food of course but . . . He sniffed the steam
pouring out of the kettle.

"Mutton, onions, garlic, turnips, rice . . ." One
by one he named what he could smell cooking. He
stood by the kettle to enjoy it. He looked around to
see if anyone was there who might offer to treat him.
No. Only a stranger eating chulaw-kabab, the tea-
house owner with a stern face for loiterers who had
no money, and Mullah Nasr-ed-Din snoring com-
fortably on the rug-covered wooden bench under the
grape arbor.

The bread Abdul Ali carried seemed dry and taste-
less as he breathed the delicious steam of the stew.
Quietly he held his loaf over the kettle, letting it
soak up the good flavors that were being wasted as the
steam melted into the air — meat, onions, garlic,
turnips, rice. Then he sat down to his feast on the
rug-covered bench next to the one where Mullah
Nasr-ed-Din was sleeping.

His stew-flavored bread was delicious. It no longer
tasted of coarse grains with a bit of sand left in. It
tasted of meat, onions, garlic, turnips and rice. He

ate it slowly. He wanted every bit of taste from each noisy mouthful of it. He wished that he had two loaves of bread instead of one to sop up the steam that poured from the kettle. Abdul Ali was smacking his lips over the last crumb of his steam-soaked bread when Masud, the tea-house owner, came up to him with hand outstretched, thumb and forefinger rubbing together.

"Now you must pay what you owe me," demanded Masud.

"What *I* owe *you?*" repeated Abdul Ali in a voice so loud that Mullah Nasr-ed-Din woke up and rubbed the sleep from his eyes.

"You must pay for the steam of my stew!" said Masud.

"The steam of your stew?" shouted Abdul Ali in a voice so sharp that Mullah Nasr-ed-Din sat up, wide awake and curious to know what was happening.

"Of course!" Masud rubbed thumb and forefinger together in the money-please sign. "You ate the steam of my good stew — meat, onions, garlic, turnips, rice. Now you must pay for it."

Abdul Ali shook his fists. He stamped his feet and moaned. He was desperate and very angry. He had no money to pay for the steam. He told Masud so in every strong word that he knew. But there stood the tea-house owner, rubbing thumb and forefinger together. Suddenly Abdul Ali saw something that made him feel better. Mullah Nasr-ed-Din was awake.

"Good Mullah," Abdul Ali appealed to him, "you heard what happened. You are the one to judge between us. Must a hungry man pay for steam?"

"Yes, Mullah," agreed Masud. "Whatever you say will be right. Tell us. Does Abdul Ali owe money for the steam of my stew made of meat, onions, garlic, turnips and rice?"

Mullah Nasr-ed-Din stroked his beard and looked very wise. While he thought and thought, Masud and Abdul Ali tried to outshout one another. Each gave his own side of the story. Finally the Mullah held up his hand for silence. Masud and Abdul Ali waited for the words that would settle their dispute.

"What do you charge for your steam, Masud?" asked the Mullah.

The tea-house owner named a price that would have made his richest customer bargain for a lower one.

"I will pay the bill for Abdul Ali," the Mullah told the two surprised men. "Masud charged enough for a full bowl of stew, but I will pay it for the steam that flavored Abdul Ali's bread."

The Mullah pulled his money bag from his wide gaily-colored belt. He counted out the three coins Masud had demanded. Then he did a most surprising thing. He stood on his bench and held the coins high in the air. One by one he let them drop to the ground. Clink! Clink! Clink!

Masud stooped to pick up the coins, but the Mullah was faster. He jumped from his bench and scooped the money back into his bag, which he tucked firmly inside his belt.

"What are you doing with my money?" shouted Masud.

"Your money? It is my money. You have had your pay." The Mullah settled back on his bench to finish the nap that had been interrupted. "Steam and sound are two of a kind, floating on the air like brothers. The sound of the money has paid you well for the steam of your stew."

THE SPECIALIST

WHEN Mullah Nasr-ed-Din climbed down from his donkey's back at Masud's tea house, there was something bulky under his long priestly robes. When he sat down on the Persian rug that softened the hard boards of the cot-sized bench in front of the tea house, something long stuck out from under his dark overcoat.

"A glass of tea, please," he ordered from the tea-house owner. He stroked his beard contentedly. A sparrow chirped in the grapevine of the arbor over his head. Men and children gathered as they always did when their Mullah sat down, relaxed and chatty. Women hovered as close as they could without seeming bold.

"Salam!" he exchanged greetings with them. He put a lump of sugar between his teeth and sipped his hot tea in loud satisfying gulps. They talked about the weather, the locusts, and the low price of wheat.

The villagers eyed the bulky something under the Mullah's robes, but asked no questions. They saw the pleased-with-himself expression on the Mullah's face and knew that he had something to show them when he was ready. Persian villagers at a tea house on a hot summer day are never in a hurry. The crowd grew bigger and more friendly with every glass of tea.

Setting down his empty glass, the Mullah pulled from under his robes a tar, a stringed instrument that is a little like a big mandolin and a little like a guitar. The tea-house sitters were delighted. They loved music and there was little of it in their village except what they made with their own voices.

"We did not know you could play the tar," said the people, admiring him.

The Mullah's mysterious smile seemed to say, "I have many skills you do not know!"

Sitting cross-legged on the rug-covered bench, he held himself straight, tall and proud. He pressed the tar firmly against his chest with his left hand, just as he had watched the Shah's musicians do. He pressed the strings firmly with his left hand while he strummed the strings vigorously with his right hand.

"Zing, zing, zing!" sang the tar, repeating the same note over and over. "Zing, zing, zing!"

Men left their tables and their benches to crowd around the Mullah. Children stopped wading in the ditch to stand and gape at him. Women's dark eyes peered from their chuddars as they joined the listeners. The sparrow stopped chirping in the grapevine and cocked a bright eye toward the new sound.

"Zing, zing, zing!" the note repeated itself as the Mullah strummed with his right hand and pressed the same spot on the same string with his left hand. People began to laugh, to clap their hands over their ears, and to jest about the Mullah's playing. On and on he played the same note, "Zing, zing, zing!" And as he played his bearded chin went higher in the air, so pleased was he with the music he was making.

"Mullah Nasr-ed-Din!" It was Masud, the owner of the tea house, whose ears tired first. "There are other strings on your tihar. There are other places to press that one string you are using. Why don't you move your fingers up and down? That is what other players do."

"Zing, zing, zing," came from the Mullah's tar, making a monotonous accompaniment to his answer. "I know how others play. Their groping fingers wander up and down the strings. They seem always to be hunting for a tone they cannot find. Poor men! I pity them their restless, searching way of playing. They are never satisfied. They never find the right note."

"Zing, zing, zing!" twanged the Mullah's tar as his fingers firmly pressed the same spot. "Now I," bragged the Mullah. "I have found the note I want. My search is over. I am perfecting this one note that is exactly right. I am a specialist."

The crowd murmured in admiration. "The perfect note! The Mullah is a specialist!" Then they went back to their naps, or their tea, or their play as the Mullah sat alone on his rug-covered bench, twanging his perfect note — "Zing, zing, zing!" And overhead the sparrow began chirping again.

TOO HEAVY

ONCE the Mullah rode his little donkey to the vegetable bazaar. His own garden did not grow every kind of vegetable that Fatima wanted for her stew. The market was colorful with its piles of purple eggplant, green cabbages, and yellow melons. It was fun bargaining with the farmers who were his good friends. Before he knew it, the Mullah had bought more than Fatima had ordered. The vegetables stretched the bag he had brought. He loaded the heavy beets and melons in the bottom, the medium-weight eggplant and cabbage in the middle, and the tender herbs on top. He stooped under the weight of the bag as he dragged it toward his sleepy donkey. For a minute he stood beside the donkey, looking at her and thinking.

She braced her small feet, expecting him to load the saddlebags as usual. Instead he whispered into her long twitching ears, "How tiny you are!" Then he climbed on the donkey's back, holding the bag of vegetables out at arm's length. He sat, as he often did, facing backward to be polite to the friends he was leaving behind in the bazaar. He clucked to the donkey and started jogging through the village streets toward home. His legs swung loosely at the donkey's side. He held the vegetables stiffly at arm's length, first with one hand, then with the other, and then with both. He rode so awkwardly that women

peered at him from behind their chuddars and boys laughed heartily.

His pupil Shoja the baker's son stared at him. "Why are you carrying your bag that way?" he asked. "Why don't you put your vegetables in the donkey's saddlebags where they belong?"

"Oh no!" the Mullah hurried to reply. "These vegetables are heavy and my donkey is small. It would be too much of a load for the donkey to carry the bag and me too. So I carry the vegetables, and the donkey carries me."

Shoja stood scratching his head, trying to understand, while the Mullah rode on toward home, holding his bag of vegetables out at arm's length, and feeling very happy that he could save his good donkey the extra burden.

GLOSSARY

THE words marked * have been adopted into the English language. Their dictionary spelling is used even when it does not exactly represent their sound in Persian. The word *mullah,* for instance, is pronounced more like *molla.*

The unmarked words are spelled as they sound. Stress every syllable.

*Agha: mister, a term of respect

ah wahi: an exclamation of distress

ai anar: the call of a pomegranate seller. *Ai* is to get the buyer's attention. *Anar* is the name of the fruit.

*Allah: the Arabic name for God

*chuddar: the all-covering shawl worn by all Persian women in olden times. Today it is worn by some women.

chulaw-kabab: a favorite dish of rice and meat

135

*dinar: a small coin formerly used in Persia
*kismet: fate or destiny
*Koran: the sacred book of the Mohammedans
mast: clabbered milk or yoghurt
*minaret: the mosque tower from which the call to
     prayer is given
*mosque: the building where Mohammedans meet
     for worship
*muezzin: the priest who gives the call to prayer
*mullah: a Mohammedan official who acts as priest,
     teacher, and judge
*pilau: rice cooked in broth of meat or vegetables
puh! puh!: an exclamation of displeasure
*salam: a greeting meaning "peace"
*Shah: the king of Persia
*tar: a musical instrument, a lute

ACKNOWLEDGMENTS

As stated in the foreword, these stories were told by many persons in Iran. Though it is impossible to list their names, sincere gratitude goes to all who shared their knowledge of Mullah Nasr-ed-Din.

The quotations on pages 51, 97, 108 and 109 are from *The Holy Koran* as translated by Professor A. J. Arberry. These are used by permission of George Allen and Unwin, London, and Macmillan Company, New York.

Some of the stories in this book appeared first in magazines. Thanks for their use are due the publishers of *American Junior Red Cross News, Highlights for Children, Jack and Jill, Pulpit Digest, Trailblazer, Trails for Juniors,* and *World Youth.*

The Fantastic Fruit Group

Aboff

by Gary Swift

FIRST GRAPHiCS